MW00879840

TALES FROM THE LAND OF NO MONDAYS

JIM MORRIS

AND

DAN SULLIVAN

This is a special edition, first run, hardback version of

Tales From The Land of No Mondays.

No manatees were injured in the production of this special edition, but the publisher did fall off his barstool and spill his beer.

When a songwriter and an author spend time together fishing, drinking, and telling stories, the results can be dubious.

Tales from The Land of No Mondays

Published on a barstool in the U.S.A by:

Old Stone Publishing
Boise, ID 83714
info@oldstonepublishing.com
First Edition
ISBN: 978-1-54896-369-9

Printed in the United States of America

All characters in this publication are entirely fictitious. Any resemblance to real persons, living or dead, is purely coincidental, unless you recognize your name or anecdotes, in which case I warned you that it wasn't safe to drink with me.

FOREWORD

Tales from the Land of No Mondays is more than a story; it's a fantastic voyage, a mostly fictional story about a man's journey from the drudgery of a corporate career to finally living the dream of doing what he loved, singing and telling stories in paradise.

To the casual reader, it is a fun read with some occasionally quirky, rhyming story lines. To his fans, *Tales* is a wonderful ride through the stories, the songs, and the lyrics of Jim Morris.

When Jim left us, he took with him a tremendous amount of talent, hundreds of new song ideas, and some of the novel that he and Dan Sullivan spoke of writing.

Thanks to Dan for stepping in and finishing this book, using more than eighty of Jim's songs to create a wonderful novel. Also, thanks to Dave Monahan, Vido and Jodi, Dennis and Nancy and the gang at the Nav-A-Gator, Laura, Beth, and everybody else who had a hand in this this project. And special thanks to all of you, Jim's amazing friends and fans for the outpouring of love and support over the years.

Sharon Morris
Burnt Store Marina
September, 2017

CHAPTER ONE

I've Got This Really Good Tequila in my Room

He was never going to drink again. The sun stabbed him in the eye through a gap left in the blinds. Even with his eyes closed, it felt like he was staring into the headlights of an approaching train. A collision with a train seemed oddly comforting; it would put an end to his hangover.

He rolled over to escape the beam of sunlight and became aware of another body in his bed. Opening his eyes, he was shaken to see a freaky face, inches from his own, with a disproportionately large nose. Her mouth was slightly opened, revealing what appeared to be buck teeth, and her breath smelled like a New Orleans street corner after a long Saturday night. He jerked back a foot or so and blinked his eyes several times to bring the face into focus. She was actually quite attractive from a more distant perspective.

What was her name? He slowly pulled a pillow over his face while trying to put together the pieces of an evening gone awry. Snippets of the previous day started to come to him through the fog. He was in St. Louis for a conference. He had skipped the afternoon session on the last day and dropped by the hotel bar to decide what to do with his newfound freedom.

He remembered the pretty woman sitting alone at the corner table. She had smiled at him when their eyes met. It was that certain smile, that right kind of smile, the one that said it was okay to approach her. The bar was nearly empty, but he had acted like there wasn't an open chair in the entire place. He looked around for a seat as he moved in her direction. "Is this seat taken?" he asked while pointing to the chair across from her.

She had smiled and laughed, saying, "I've been saving it for you. It's about time you got here. Everybody's been after that chair. I'm ... Can I buy you a drink?"

What was her name? She was in town for a wedding and was from somewhere out west. Oregon? Nevada? She had bought him a couple glasses of very expensive Pappy Van Winkle's Family Reserve, ordering it neat. "Ice is for sissies," she told him, and he certainly didn't want to come across as a sissy, even though he rarely drank bourbon or whiskey. Beer and rum were his drinks of choice and he wished now that he had stuck to them. He drank the free whiskey and he chased it with beer. They drank and laughed and then she invited him upstairs because she had some really good tequila in her room.

Jack was three years out of college, a damn good engineer who worked hard all day but loved to party the night away when he had the chance. He thought the St. Louis conference would be a simple distraction from his job. It was a chance to get away from his desk and away from the monotony that his job had become in just a few short years. And he felt that he was getting a little deserved payback from his company, something he felt they owed him for his upcoming transfer.

A few months after graduating from Georgia Tech with a degree in Mechanical Engineering, he had accepted a position with a medium-sized engineering firm, Baxter and Hutton. He was placed in their regional office on St. Simons Island.

Only a few years later, Jack felt trapped by his job and by the constraints of a career. The pay was rewarding, but the job wasn't satisfying. He dreamed of throwing it all away and moving south to some beach where he could play his guitar for tips at some funky little bar, occasionally take tourists fishing, and spend his free time lying by the water, simply enjoying life. That would be satisfying but probably not rewarding.

Despite the drudgery of his job, Jack's original plan had been working out just fine. He was young, talented, making good money, single, and planned to stay that way as long as he could, avoiding kids and a wife. Between St. Simons and the communities across the causeway on the mainland, Jack had a seemingly endless supply of young women to drive crazy with his carefree approach to dating and relationships. It really had been the three best years of his life.

The throbbing headache stabbed at his brain, his mouth was dry, his stomach hurt, and he had to move. He carefully reached for her arm and slid it off his shoulder, then slipped out from underneath the covers. He found his underwear behind the chair in the corner, his pants and shirt were near the door where they had fallen, and his shoes were fifteen feet apart: one near the door, the other across the room.

"Sneaking out?" she asked in a quiet, raspy voice.

"No," Jack lied. "I was going to go find us some breakfast and a couple of mimosas."

"Hmmm," she said as she pulled the sheets over her naked body, "that sounds good."

What was her name?

Escaping to the hallway, Jack eased the door closed as quietly as he could. He noted her room number, 302, then started his walk of shame, carrying his shoes down the hallway towards the elevator and his room on the fifth floor.

***

The knocking on her hotel room door intensified to an impatient pounding before Mary Jane finally gave up and yelled, "I'm coming!" She got out of bed and looked around the room for her shirt and pants. She was relieved that she was alone.

"Who is it?" she asked as she got to the door, hoping it wasn't Jack returning with breakfast and hopes of a replay of last night.

"It's Jenny," came the angry reply. "Open the damn door."

Mary Jane opened the door to find her best friend with an all too familiar "pissed off" look on her face.

"Jesus," Jenny said as she pushed her way into the room. Mary Jane's hair was a matted mess, and the room smelled of booze, sweat, and sex. Half empty bottles and clothes were strewn about. Signs of human wreckage were everywhere.

"What or who in the hell happened to you last night?" asked Jenny. "You look like shit. You missed my rehearsal, my rehearsal dinner, and you didn't return my calls. What the hell is going through your head?"

"I'm sorry," said Mary Jane, although she wasn't really. "I guess I drank a little too much and fell asleep."

"Fell asleep with who? Where is the scumbag de jour?" asked Jenny in an angry tone. "We've got a hair and nails appointment in an hour. Do you think you can pull yourself together long enough to be my maid of honor or are you too busy drinking and screwing yourself into oblivion?"

"I'm sorry, Jenny," she said with all the false sincerity that she could muster. "I'll be downstairs in forty-five minutes."

Mary Jane closed the door and took a hard-right turn into the bathroom. She dropped her clothes on the floor, stepped into the shower, and turned it on cold. Her entire body hurt. When she put her head under the shower water, she swore that even her hair hurt. Her attempt to lose herself and her problems in booze and sex had failed as she had known it would. It had always been that way.

In a few hours, she would be the maid of honor at her best friend's wedding. The problem was that she had always loved the groom. Jenny and Mary Jane had grown up next door to each other in the northern Nevada town of Fallon. They were best friends from the moment they could crawl, and they had shared everything: clothes, money, and deep secrets.

They met Bill in first grade and the three of them quickly became known as the Three Musketeers. They were inseparable friends. In high school, they dated others, they had other friends, but they never lost the moniker and everybody agreed there could never be a tighter group of friends than the Three Musketeers.

Mary Jane had always loved Bill. From the day she had met him, she knew in her heart that one day she would marry him. He was her destiny.

After high school, Mary Jane went to Carroll College in Helena, Montana on an academic scholarship while Bill and Jenny both ended up at University of Nevada, Reno. The three continued to get together every chance they could get, and when they did, it was as if not a single day had been missed. They were as tight as ever. Even when Bill was dating that rich cheerleader, Mary Jane knew that she and Bill would live their lives in Fallon, raise their children, and grow old together. It was, unfortunately, the only secret she had never told Jenny.

Their junior year of college, tragedy struck when Bill's father was killed in a strange blender accident, making frozen drinks one day. Mary Jane rushed home for the funeral, and both girls stayed by their friend's side for several days. Mary Jane promised she would call him from Montana to check in every day and she did for more than a month. Their friendship grew even stronger. At the same time, Jenny was doing her best to comfort him as well. She was spending as much time as she could with him, letting him cry on her shoulder, comforting him in any way she could.

It was during this time when Bill and Jenny's relationship gradually changed. Before they knew it, they each started having romantic feelings for the other. They both, in their own ways, attributed it to the emotions of the situation, but eventually, neither could ignore their feelings and their friendship erupted into a full-fledged relationship.

Mary Jane was still undeterred. She spoke with both of them on a regular basis and knew that this was just a brief romance. They were victims of life's circumstances and she prayed that when it ended, it wouldn't break up the Three Musketeers. She still believed that Bill would be her man. In her mind, nothing could change that eventuality.

After college, Jenny was offered a job in St. Louis and Bill followed her, finding a career there as well. Mary Jane went back to Fallon to take a position in human resources with Northrop Grumman. She was still somewhat confident that Bill and Jenny would break up, still pinning her hopes on Bill.

To fill her time, she dated a succession of losers. The only kind of man that she ever wanted, however, were the ones that she knew she couldn't hold very long, because Bill was still her destiny. She bided her time, dating idiots and working for bureaucrats. She discovered over time that she really didn't care much for the corporate world. She also found that Fallon was a very, very small town.

The phone call came one Saturday night after Mary Jane got home from a bad date. Bill and Jenny were so excited to tell her the news of their engagement. They wanted her to act as both his best man and her maid of honor. The Three Musketeers would stand united—or some bullshit like that—they had said.

Mary Jane took the news admirably. She congratulated them and told them they should probably rethink their attendant plan, then hung up and cried her way through two bottles of wine. She had become another victim of romance. She spent most of Sunday throwing up and called in sick on Monday.

* * *

Finding his way back to his own hotel room, Jack collapsed on the bed. He felt awful, but pieces of his drunken night with

What's-her-name were coming back to him and that gave him a little smile.

It was probably an evening they both needed. He was about to be transferred from a life he loved on St. Simons Island to Wilmington, Delaware. While he had never actually been to Delaware, it sounded absolutely horrible. It snowed there, every winter. Jack didn't want to sound like a wimp, but seventy-five was pretty chilly to him. He would be leaving behind everything and everybody he knew, and for what? A job?

Over the whiskey, she told him about the wedding that she had dreaded for so long. The bride was her best friend, but she had always loved the groom. She told him that she could really use a friend, and that she didn't want to offend him or to assume, but she had this really good tequila in her room upstairs.

Jack hadn't planned to leave the bar with the girl. He felt like he would be taking advantage of her, but when he shared his plight with her, she smiled and said, "I know what would fix you right up. Good tequila and a quick roll in the hay." How could any man argue with that logic?

After a two-hour nap, an order of pancakes from room service, and a long shower with a beer from the honor bar, Jack started feeling human again. He couldn't say he felt good, but well enough to make his flight home. He packed his bag and walked to the elevator. He pressed the "Lobby" button, and then on a whim, pressed the button for the third floor. He walked to her room and knocked, but there was no answer.

In the lobby, he checked out without even glancing at his bill. As he started towards the door, a group of women were coming in with their hair all done like women do for weddings, pulled up high, pieces of baby's breath sticking out here and there, and a big bun on top. The third woman through the door was "her." The moment Jack saw her face, Mary Jane's name came back to him. They stared at each other for a moment, then Jack motioned with a nod of his head to meet him over at the side of the lobby.

"I'll catch up with you guys," Mary Jane said to the bridal party. The other girls shot Jack glances ranging from curiosity to knowing smirks to irritation. He heard somebody whisper "That's him" as they walked away.

"I think I'm supposed to tell you that I had a really good time last night," said Jack with an uncomfortable grin.

"It was fun," said Mary Jane with a slight smile. "If you ever find yourself in Nevada, look me up."

Jack looked at the floor for a moment before raising his eyes to meet hers. "Hey, do me quick favor. Quickly look across the lobby and count how many times you see the color red."

"What?" asked Mary Jane.

"Just humor me. In five seconds, count how many different places you see the color red."

Mary Jane glanced across the lobby for a moment, then nodded to him, "Okay."

"Now close your eyes," said Jack.

"What?"

"Just close your eyes," Jack repeated. Mary Jane gave him a slightly irritated look but then closed her eyes. "Now tell me how many different places you saw the color blue."

Mary Jane opened her eyes with a grin. "You said red."

Jack smiled. "Right. I said 'red,' so you never noticed the color blue. You've been so absorbed by a preconceived notion from your childhood of who you were going to marry that you've never been able to see anything else. You've been so focused on what you believed your life would be that you never looked around to see what it could be. You've concentrated so blindly on red that you've never noticed the color blue."

She stared at him, wanting to argue, but no words came to her lips. Jack leaned over, kissed her on the forehead, and walked out the door to a waiting taxi. Mary Jane stood in silence and watched the taxi, and Jack, drive out of sight.

***

Jack smiled as the plane lifted off the runway at Lambert Field. It had been a pretty good trip. He had enjoyed a couple of nice meals, shared a crazy night with a pretty girl, and actually learned a couple of things that would help him in his job. His smile dissolved when he realized that in a week he would be moving to Wilmington Fucking Delaware. He laid his head back against the seat and tried to sleep.

CHAPTER TWO

The Wedding She Had Dreaded for So Long

The wedding was right out of the Lutheran wedding manual, if such a thing existed. It hadn't mattered that Mary Jane had missed the rehearsal, she had it down pat. Traditional music to walk slowly up the aisle with Bill's cousin, traditional music for the clad-in-white bride to march up to the altar, and a wedding mass full of ritual and light on anything that really had to do with Bill and Jenny.

What struck Mary Jane was the abundance of red that she noticed. Bill was wearing a black tux with a red bow tie and vest and his face seemed to be flushed and red. The carnations in Jenny's bouquet were a bright shade of red, the Bible was red, the lady in the third row had a red hat. She found herself desperately looking for blue, just to symbolically prove to herself that she could see it. Uncle Ted wore a navy blazer, she noted. Good enough.

Since Jack had walked out of the hotel, his analogy of red and blue had been stuck firmly in her head. Something mighty had made a right-hand turn into her world. She was very angry with that asshole from Georgia for suggesting that she couldn't see the forest for the trees, yet at the same time, she was standing two steps below the altar, picking up the pieces of her hopes and dreams.

At the reception, she feigned her best smile and gave a brief speech about how she always knew the bride and groom were perfect for each other. She toasted them with champagne, danced with the pervert who said he was Jenny's uncle on her mother's side, and she threw birdseed at the newly married couple when they ran out of the hall and got into Bill's red Volvo for their ten-minute ride to a hotel on the Interstate. She caught a ride back to the hotel with a chain-smoking, much older cousin who offered to buy her a drink in the bar. She declined.

Back in her room, she shed the awful bridesmaid dress and the wrong-sized, horribly uncomfortable bra. She pulled on a t-shirt, a pair of shorts, and her flip-flops. She stuffed everything she owned, except for the dress, which she left crumpled on the floor, into her roller bag, and headed for her rental car.

***

Jack's relatively short flight home included a brief layover in Chicago. As he sat at the gate waiting to board the second leg to Savannah, he remembered that an old college friend lived in the area and that he had her number jotted down in the little notebook he carried with him. He called the number, and after three rings, he got a generic voicemail message that simply stated that he had reached such and such number and please leave a message. After the beep, hoping it was still her number, he said, "Hi, Karen, it's Jack. I'm in Chicago and I don't get here that much. I'm just passing through and I thought of you, so I tried to get in touch. I hope my sudden phone call doesn't seem too weird. I just thought I'd let you know that I haven't disappeared."

He hung up the phone thinking about his strange message to Karen, then grabbed a pen and his boarding pass and started writing down what he had just said. It sort of sounded like the lyrics to a song. As he boarded the plane, the gate agent took his boarding pass and the words to the first song he had ever written.

***

Mary Jane didn't know where she was going; she was just driving. Her rental car wasn't due back for a day and she had a day to kill before her return flight to Reno. Not wanting to hang around the hotel, she just drove.

She experienced a wild range of emotions. One moment, she cried, thinking that she would never find happiness; the next, she would feel strangely calm, happy that the wedding was over, and she was at peace. Moments later, she would feel a wave of freedom, the open road, nothing holding her back, and then she would end up sobbing again.

The contrast of her emotions was like the two billboards she saw on I-70. The sign on the left said, “Jesus is Lord, Make Him Your Savior Today.” The sign on the right said, “We Dare to Bare All, Stop in at Café Risqué.” She was totally conflicted as she drove down the Interstate. It was the crazy duality of life: she was free to live her life any way she wanted, and at the same time, had never been so sad.

After four hours of wandering, she found herself in the tiny town of Monroe City, Missouri, out of gas, hungry, and tired. She drove down the main drag looking for a place to eat. She pulled into what appeared to be the most happening place in town, a white building that had probably been an auto dealership in another life, now a bar called The Dugout.

She took a seat at the bar next to an older gentleman wearing a ball cap and a red flannel shirt who had a half glass of beer sitting in front of him. He stared up at the baseball game on the TV above the bar. She liked crusty old men. They reminded her of her grandfather, who had passed away several years earlier. “What are you drinking?” she asked, pointing to the man’s beer.

“A Pabst,” he said with kind of a snort.

“Two PBRs,” she said to the bartender as he passed by. The old man gave her a quick glance, then turned back towards the baseball game on the TV.

She laughed when she noticed the menu above the bar. The price for a glass of beer was cheaper than the price for a bottle of water. When the beers arrived, the man finished his half beer in two swallows and pushed the empty glass across the bar. He picked up the fresh beer and turned towards her with it raised to clink together with hers. "Thanks. I'm Howard."

"Well hi, Howard. I'm Mary Jane."

"New here in town?" he asked.

"No," she said with a pause. "Just passing through."

He took a sip of his beer. "Going to?"

Mary Jane laughed, then took a swig of her beer. "I don't know where I'm going."

Howard smiled. "Well, if you don't know where you're going, any road will get you there."

"That's a good point," she said.

Howard looked at her for a moment before asking, "Why is a pretty girl like you in a place like this talking to a guy like me?"

"You don't talk to girls?" Mary Jane asked with a grin.

"Well, they don't come wandering in off the street and buy me beer too much anymore."

"Well, Howard, I guess it's your lucky day. How's the food here?"

***

After an uneventful flight to Savannah, Jack found his Jeep in the airport lot and made the trip down I-95 to his little house on St. Simons in just over an hour. He tossed his luggage on the bed, found some left-over, week-old pizza in the fridge, and mixed himself a tall rum drink. After choking down the pizza, he refreshed his drink, grabbed his old guitar, and retreated to the front porch to put his feet up and reminisce about his life in Georgia.

Jack had never lived outside of his home state. He should have been thinking of the move to Delaware as a new and exciting adventure, but the over-powering emotion was simply one of dread. He understood all the selling points his boss had used to make the move sound attractive. Working at corporate headquarters would give him valuable exposure to the company leaders, he would be living in a growing, vibrant city, and he would be working on larger, more exciting projects. But in Jack's eyes, anything north of Myrtle Beach was just too damn cold, summer or winter.

He strummed his guitar under the single exposed light bulb on the porch and tried to remember the lyrics he wrote on his boarding pass. He reminisced about his years in Georgia and his childhood. Playing the guitar at night on his porch often reminded him of his neighbor Tom, the old man who lived behind them when he was growing up. In his mind, he could see him playing every night in the halo of his back-porch light. Jack and his friends, Charlie and Randy, always had referred to him as Old Man Tom, but not to his face.

If you sat and listened, Old Man Tom would aggressively share the wisdom of his years and if you promised not to tell your parents, he would even give you a swallow of his beer. When he drank too much, his songs got slow, his eyes turned red, and his voice got low. He would sing about some woman he loved in New Orleans.

Tom was a retired army man, a veteran of three wars. Jack's friend Charlie used to say that he bet Old Man Tom could talk until doomsday and never tell the same tale twice. He was a great story-teller, and they loved to listen to his tales. Jack never forgot one piece of advice he received from Tom. "Learn to play that guitar, son. You'll always have a friend."

Tom had left town in quite a hurry. Jack came home from school one day and his mom told him he had gone, but he had left Jack a note which read, "Sorry I couldn't say goodbye, but I couldn't miss my chance. They tell me that her husband died. I'm off to find romance, Tom." Jack kept the little piece of paper tucked away in the back of his favorite Hardy Boys mystery book. He always thought it sounded like a song.

Jack never knew what happened to Old Man Tom; by now, he was probably long dead. But every time he went down to New Orleans, he would think about the old man with the guitar and the endless string of advice and opinions. He couldn't help but to look for his face, sitting in a backstreet bar or in an old lawn chair on the porch of a small house.

Jack remembered everything Tom had told him, and as he got older, he started to realize what some of it meant. Tom had told him, "Always keep life simple, like an old familiar song. But if it ever got too familiar, just make it up as you go along." That piece of advice was making more sense to him all the time.

Jack hadn't spent much time thinking about his childhood over the years, but he remembered that it had been a great time to grow up. When he could get his nose out of some mystery book, he and Charlie had grand adventures. Charlie was a dreamer. Jack had met him back in school and they became good friends along the way. Charlie's lively imagination led them to play pilot from the old magnolia tree, shooting down the enemy fighter planes one by one. They built tree houses, swam in Charlie's pond, or pretended to be Mickey Mantle, hitting rocks in the field by the road. They would live out the adventures they read about in Hardy Boys books or play Napoleon Solo from The Man from U.N.C.L.E. There was seldom a boring day when Charlie was around.

In high school, Jack and Charlie had drifted away from each other but still remained friends. After graduation, Jack was accepted to Georgia Tech and Charlie joined the army. "I'm off to fight the war," he said. Before he left for basic training that summer, Jack ran into him and made a comment about how it didn't seem fair that he would be at school with pretty girls and kegs of beer while Charlie would be hunkered down in some foxhole with a bunch of sweaty soldiers.

Charlie's smile went away as he kicked the dirt, saying, "That's the way it happens, there's so much you can't control.

I'm getting out of here, but I tell you man, one day I'm going for the gold."

Every now and then, Jack would hear a crazy tale about some exotic place where Charlie had been seen. Some folks said he was rich, some said that he was in jail, but Jack always guessed the truth was somewhere in between.

***

Howard and Mary Jane talked for nearly two hours as she ate half of the huge tenderloin sandwich that he had suggested. Howard ate the other half. He was a retired, third-generation farmer. His plan had always been to hand the family rutabaga farm down to his two sons, but his youngest went to college and became a physical therapist in Kansas City. His older boy was a "worthless piece of shit."

After Howard's wife died, he sold the farm his family had owned for almost a hundred years. He bought a little place in town and spent his mornings in the coffee shop with the other farmers. Most afternoons, he was over at Robie's Hardware store chewing the fat with customers and a bunch of other old boys who hung out there, and he usually stopped by the bar for a beer on the way home.

Mary Jane was almost giddy. It was as if she was talking to her grandpa. He spoke slowly and plainly, and seemed as honest as the day was long. She felt she could tell him anything, and after a few beers, she did.

When she finished the condensed version of her love life, Howard took a pull off his beer and looked at her for a long while with a furrowed brow. Finally, he said, "You're like ol' Shorty Watkins over there. Man's been pissed off at me for three years 'cause I sold my big tractor to another feller. He wanted to buy it from me but never told me. Did you ever mention to this fella that you wanted to marry him?"

"Not exactly," she said after turning back towards her beer.

"Then what do you or Shorty have to be angry about? I know for sure I ain't a mind reader, and I'll bet this boy who married the other gal ain't either."

She knew he was right. It was exactly the kind of logic her grandfather would have dispensed and while it wasn't the truth she wanted to hear, it was what she needed someone to tell her. The two of them sat there sipping their beers for a few minutes before she turned to him and asked, "Howard, what is the bluest thing you've ever seen in your entire life?"

He looked up towards the now dark TV screen for a thoughtful moment. "A few years before she died, me and the wife took a drive down to the Florida Keys. I'd have to say that the ocean down there, on a sunny day, is just about the bluest thing I ever saw in my whole life."

"Don't laugh," said Mary Jane, "but I've never seen the ocean."

***

Jack woke up, alone and in his own bed, but experiencing his second hangover in two days. Maybe it was time to start rethinking his life. Today's rum hangover wasn't nearly as bad as the previous day's. Thankfully, it was Sunday. He crawled out of bed, made a pot of coffee, and with a cup in hand, walked out onto the front porch where the single light bulb still glowed and his old guitar still leaned against the side of the house. He shook his head; he couldn't believe he had left his guitar out all night.

Sitting in the old green lawn chair, he looked out across the street towards the water. Between the houses, under the live oak trees, from just the spot he was sitting, he could see the water two blocks away. "Ocean View" were the two words that had attracted him to check out this rental. It was a stretch, but he couldn't deny that he could see the water from this one particular spot on the porch, and from his vantage point, it looked calm and blue and beautiful.

He needed to start packing for his move, but he really wanted to go to the beach. He wanted to spend a few hours floating a cooler full of beer and drinking waist-deep in the water with friends. His beach days were numbered, incredibly numbered. He reached for his guitar and started to strum, nothing in particular, just some old familiar chords.

The old island looked different to him. Nothing had changed, but his leaving made everything seem more vibrant; everywhere he looked was like a picture from a magazine. He reached for a pen on the ground next to the little table. A week-old newspaper still sat on the table under a small rock. Reaching over his guitar and using his knee as a desk, he made notes on the margins of the paper: a poem, a song? Perhaps it was a love letter to St. Simons Island. He jotted down his favorite memories of his island days. He asked himself how could he leave here? He needed to find a way to get blown off course; he needed to find a way to stay. Maybe he could be a bartender. He wondered how much it paid.

***

Mary Jane felt like a bird just released from an entire life in a cage. She still had feelings and emotions for Bill, but for the first time since hearing the news of their engagement, she knew she would get over him eventually. She knew that an exciting life was ahead of her, not the predictable life she had planned and hoped for, but a new, exciting, unwritten, uncharted life full of adventure and romance and lust.

After enjoying her first restful night in six months, she drove two hours back towards St. Louis. Before turning in her rental car, she stopped at a small used car lot off I-70 and made John Treharne, the owner of Treharne Fine Motors, a very happy man. She bought a seventeen-year-old rusty blue BMW convertible that had just over 175,000 miles on the odometer. John never thought he'd sell it.

Treharne followed her to the airport to drop off her rental, and just like that, she was off. There were still a few details that needed to be worked out. She would have to call her boss to let her know she wouldn't be back for another week or so, and other than her credit card, she was pretty much out of money. She needed to stop and get a map. Beyond knowing she needed to head generally south and east, she didn't know the best route to get where she was going, but she was on a mission. She had a clearly defined goal and details weren't going to derail her plan. Mary Jane was going to Key West.

She had a sunshine smile ever since she left St. Louis. A little taste of freedom, now the girl was going to go wild. She was winging east on I-64 at 75 miles-an-hour with the top down in her new-to-her BMW convertible. She was on a quest to prove the asshole from Georgia wrong—her life wasn't all red. She might have been on a path at one time, and she might have been unable to see other options, but all that had changed and her future was a rainbow. She was going to prove to herself that he was all wrong about her, and she was going to go see if the ocean was really that big and that blue.

***

It hadn't been the life Charlie had dreamed of as a child. By this time in his life, he was supposed to have been rich, living in a mansion somewhere with a beautiful wife, vacationing on his yacht, and spending his time managing his vast wealth. But at the same time, he didn't complain much about his lot in life. "There's so much you can't control," he would tell people. He had always considered himself a puppet on somebody else's string. Life happened and there wasn't much an old beach cowboy could do about it.

Charlie had graduated from high school but had never considered college. His parents and teachers had, without actually saying it, made it pretty clear that he wasn't college material. He was destined to be one of the worker bees in life; a factory employee, a laborer, a grunt. Suits and ties were for smart people, not for him.

He enlisted in the Army after high school, but it wasn't the life or the adventure the recruiter had described. It was a bunch of knuckleheads ordering a bunch of slackers to do meaningless tasks just to keep them busy. When his platoon finally went to war and first engaged in the action they had supposedly been trained to handle, half of them cowered like frightened puppies while the other half charged off toward the enemy with reckless abandon, completely forgetting their training. None of them were prepared to witness the brutality of war or the fragility of life. Everything changed that day. The mental scars would last their entire lives.

After the Army, Charlie had returned to his home town in Georgia and found a job at a refinery making a starting hourly wage while again being ordered around by a bunch of knuckleheads. Job after job, he would either quit or get fired. After a while, he had a reputation in town and soon there were no more job offers. He moved south into Florida, always looking for another job and dreaming of the day he would cast it all off and really go for the gold.

CHAPTER THREE

Mary Jane Goes to Key West

Mary Jane had made it to Atlanta the first day, and by sticking to the Turnpike, she made Port St. Lucie, Florida the second day. After a bland but free breakfast in the Holiday Inn lobby, she pointed her noble steed south under cloudy skies with scattered showers with one goal in mind. She immediately started seeing signs for places she had only heard about: Palm Beach, Boca Raton, Fort Lauderdale, and while tempted, she kept her goal in mind.

Occasionally through the mass of buildings to her left, she could see the water, but she tried not to look. When the sun came out, just north of Miami, she pulled to the side of the freeway and dropped the top. If she was going to go the distance, she was going to go in style.

The southern end of the Florida Turnpike ended at Florida City. At a convenience store, she filled up the car, bought a half case of beer and a couple of Slim Jims, then teased the young twenty-something boy behind the counter with a flirtatious wink and smile. She paid for everything with her credit card and walked back to her car with a smile so big that everybody else at the gas station wondered what she was up to.

Pulling back out onto the South Dixie Highway, she smiled and shouted out loud over the sound of the wind and the road, "Get ready, boys! I'm making the crawl down Duval Street tonight!" She let loose her best banshee scream.

She heard those Key West bars got a little bit rowdy. Judging by the mileage signs on the side of the road, she'd know for certain in a hundred miles. She laid the seat back a few clicks to better soak up the sun; her hair was pulled back and she was heading down US-1.

***

Charlie had moved just about as far south as he could, or as far south as he could afford. He and his girlfriend, Dalmatian, rented a secluded half acre with a singlewide mobile home that overlooked the mudflats on the western shore of Saddlebunch Keys. Charlie liked Dalmatian because she usually paid the rent. He honestly didn't know what she saw in him. He was just an old beach cowboy, barely hanging on, a little off center, and a little half gone. He was a friend to every stray dog and when he had food with him, he always shared it with them. Charlie got around on a rusty old bike; he hadn't owned a car in years. He had a koozie taped to the handlebars and he usually had it filled with beer.

When the weather was good and when he wasn't too drunk, he would rent rafts to tourists at Smathers Beach down on Key West. He also sold tiny amounts of pot, junky ditch weed, an ounce or two, or a joint or two at a time. He ran his enterprise from a lawn chair and made change from a cigar box. His rafts were so cheap that people almost had to rent one, although he would get a bit annoyed when he got too busy. If the weather wasn't good and he wasn't renting rafts, he would tell anybody who would listen, "Take a tip from me, drink yourself sunny!"

Despite his reasonably easy life, he had never given up the dream of hitting it big. He knew a couple of guys who ran drugs from someplace down south and he swore that one of these days he was going to join up with them to make some serious cash. He was going to go find his gold.

***

It wasn't until Key Largo that Mary Jane really started to understand what Howard had meant about the ocean in the Keys being the bluest thing he had ever seen. While it wasn't technically even blue, more of a blue/green, a margarita green, the size and the beauty of the ocean struck her in a way she wasn't prepared to handle. She was emotional, almost teary eyed at the sight of the beautiful water on both sides of the road. She ached to stop but pressed on towards Key West, her radio blasting a Jim Morris song.

She whizzed over Tavernier, Plantation Key, Windley Key, and onto Islamorada before hearing a line in a song about Key West that said, "Getting there slow is half the fun." She couldn't stand it anymore; she took a right turn looking for the water and ran directly into the Lorelei Restaurant and Cabana Bar. "Coincidence?" she asked herself. "Heck no." It was time for a drink.

The lunch crowd had dispersed and the place was fairly empty except for a few people at tables here and there. At the end of the bar sat a cute guy who was playing some sort of dice game with the bartender. They looked her way as she walked towards them and they both smiled. "What can I get you?" asked the bartender.

Mary Jane pondered the question for a moment before answering, "Vodka mojito, easy on the sugar."

"Make that two," said the guy with the dice. "Care to join us?" he asked.

"Sure," said Mary Jane. "What are you playing?"

The guy looked at her for a moment, then said, "We call it 'Liars Dice.' I'm sure it's got a real name. We just don't know it." He held out his hand. "I'm Rob. The guy with his hands in your drink glass is Paul." She glanced over at Paul, who was pulling a large mint stem out of one of the glasses with his fingers. He just shrugged.

“I’m Mary Jane,” she said while shaking his hand and noticing that he had the most interesting eyes—the term “blueberry eyes” came to her as she stared into them. “You have the most amazing eyes,” she said with a blush.

Paul laughed from behind the bar. “I should have warned you not to make eye contact with him.”

“Am I spellbound now?” she asked with a laugh. “Caught in his trap, mesmerized by his evil stare? Destined to strip off my clothes and give myself to him right here on the bar?”

Paul laughed at her antics. Rob tilted his head to the side, saying, “Hmm, works for me!”

She gave him a sly smile. “We’ll see.”

As they enjoyed their mojitos, Rob taught her to play Liar’s Dice and told her about the skinny little island he had adopted as his home a few years earlier. “I’ll tell you what, stick around and I’ll show you the sights. A little sightseeing, a nice dinner, a dip in the ocean. Doesn’t sound all bad, does it?”

And it didn’t sound bad to her. She seriously considered his offer, but she wanted to keep on moving down that highway in the sun. She took his phone number, stole a kiss from him, and got back on the road. A few miles southwest, she passed Teatable Key and crossed the bridge onto Matecumbe. There was beautiful water all along the narrow highway. She couldn’t keep from dreaming as she rolled along. The numbers on the mileage signs kept getting a little bit smaller as she drove, like some sort of a hypnotic countdown to her arrival in paradise.

Rob had told her about the party that happened each afternoon at Mallory Square when the sun went down and gave her the rundown on the best Key West bars to hit. She smiled, thinking, I’ll be walking tall down Duvall Street tonight.

***

There was no way Jack was going to get excited about packing for the move to Wilmington. He pulled all his luggage out of the closet and put the bags on his bed. He threw some old guitar sheet music into a box along with a small stack of his favorite books. Looking at the somewhat dismal progress, he decided to walk over to the Crab Trap for a beer. Hell, he thought, if some of his friends were there, he might even spring for a couple of plates of oysters and a bucket or two of beer.

He walked the two and a half blocks to find the restaurant and bar busy with tourists but void of any of his friends. He took one of the last seats at the bar and nodded to John Whalley, the bartender, who brought him a Red Stripe beer.

Taking a long pull off his beer, he spun his stool around and looked out over the pasty white or bright red-skinned tourists who occupied one of his favorite haunts. A very pretty lady at the third table over gave him an interesting smile, but her husband caught her in the act and glared at both of them. Jack spun his barstool back around, turning his back to them and laughing while John passed by him, smirking and shaking his head after witnessing the same scene.

Halfway through his beer, the couple from the table got up to leave. Jack glanced at the woman, who gave him a knowing, smoky look. She was probably in her mid-thirties, a blonde wearing a very tight dress that didn’t really cover her shapely body and long legs. Her husband was about the same age: balding, overweight, and grumpy.

Jack imagined that at one time they had been the high school football stud and the head cheerleader. She had kept her end of the bargain, but he had let his muscle turn to fat as his hair fell out. He probably floundered in some middle management job making just enough money to vacation on St. Simons, but not somewhere that required airline tickets. She looked like she was bored with the relationship, tired of his compliancy, and ready for a new adventure. He was angry with his lot in life and jealous of any man who looked sideways at his wife. Jack imagined what their encounter might have been if her husband hadn't been with her. He hadn't come to the bar looking for a wild evening with a married or even unmarried woman; he had just come here to drink.

"I just came here to drink," Jack said to himself. He pulled a wrinkled piece of paper from his pocket that contained a poor attempt at a packing list. Smoothing it out on the bar, he wrote down the words "I just came here to drink." Imagining the woman in the dress hitting on him, he continued to write, "Take your lips off my collar, take your hand off my thigh. And don't think I can't see how you undress me with your eyes. I know I'm looking hot, but it's not quite what you think, 'cause tonight, I just came here to drink."

John set a second beer in front of Jack as he sat back and read the words over and over to himself. A tune started to come to him, and he hummed it as he read the words. Then he started singing the words to himself. It wasn't bad. He could imagine the woman being incredibly persistent in her quest and considered his response. He wrote, "Who do you think you are wearing those perfect breasts? And how do you make them fit in such a tiny dress? And those legs, oh those legs, stop pointing them at me." Then Jack laughed out loud as he wrote the next line. "I see you're from Brazil, or at least you appear to be."

Hearing him laugh, John looked over at him. "What are you working on?"

"I think I'm writing a song," said Jack. "I'm gonna have to go home and get my guitar."

***

Up until the moment that her new-to-her car's engine died, Mary Jane had been very happy and even a bit smug about her old BMW purchase. Given that she hadn't done anything more than taking it for a quick drive around the block, it had performed brilliantly, right up until it didn't. She had coasted to a wide spot off the road, just fourteen miles short of Key West. Opening the hood, she exhausted all of her mechanical knowledge by identifying that the engine looked like an engine to her. She didn't see anything leaking, no smoke, and nothing appeared to be loose or falling off.

With her head under the car's hood, the man on the bicycle appeared suddenly beside her. His looks startled her more than his sudden arrival. He had long, straggly, unwashed hair that stuck out from under an ancient and crumpled cowboy hat. He wore a dirty flannel shirt and a pair of shorts with holes in them. His flip-flops didn't match. The cowboy's noble steed was an old ten-speed bike with the handlebars turned upside down. A koozie taped to the center of the bars held a can of beer. A rack on the back of the bike held a wooden crate filled with an assortment of "treasures."

"What's the problem?" asked the man.

Mary Jane took a step back, saying, "I don't know. It was running just fine until it died."

The man stepped off his bike and leaned it against the side of the car. "Well, let's have a look." He jiggled a few things for a minute or two, then said, "I think it's your ground wire. She's pretty loose and rusted down there."

"Is it difficult to fix?" she asked.

He reached into the bottom of the box on the back of his bike and found an adjustable wrench. "No, I should be able to fix it up in a couple of minutes."

She watched as he disconnected the cable from the engine block. Then he looked around on the ground until he found a flat rock, which he used like sandpaper on both the engine and the cable. Once he was satisfied, he blew the dust off the end of the cable and reattached it to the block.

"Okay, give her a try," he said while he finished off the beer from his handlebar koozie.

Mary Jane stepped into the car, took a deep breath, and turned the key. The engine started without a hitch. She leapt from the car. "Thank you so much!" she said with a big smile. "I have some cold beer in the trunk. Would you like one?"

The man nodded, then quietly asked, "I see you're pointed down island. Can I get a ride to Key West?"

Mary Jane paused. Her initial reaction was "hell no," but the man had just saved her on the side of the road. It was only ten or fifteen miles to Key West, she was in an open top convertible on a busy highway, and despite his scary looks, for some reason, she felt he was likely pretty harmless. "You and your bike?" she asked. He nodded and she replied, "Toss it in the backseat" as she got two cold ones out of the cooler.

Now that she was back on the road with the old hippie cowboy and a bicycle poking up from the backseat, she watched as he took a drink from his beer and held out his hand. "I'm Charlie. Some people down here call me John."

She put her beer between her legs and took his hand. "Nice to meet you, Charlie John. I'm Mary Jane."

"You can just call me Charlie or John."

She shot him a smile. "Nope, if I have to have two names, so do you. I'm going to call you Charlie John from now on."

He gave a snort and a shrug of his shoulder as he took another drink of his beer. "What brings you to the Keys?"

Mary Jane thought about it for a moment before replying, "I came down here to have a look around. I needed to get away. Why not do it somewhere as beautiful as this?"

"It's a pretty place," he said while looking out over the water to his right. "It can be intoxicating, even addictive. I came down here a couple of hundred years ago, just to look around, and I've never left."

"Tell me this," she said after a few moments. "What color would you say the water is over there, if you were to describe it to somebody who had never seen it before?"

Charlie looked over the passing bridge railing for a long time before he turned back to answer her odd question. "I'd say that was just about the bluest water I'd ever seen."

Mary Jane smiled. "That's exactly what I'd say too. What takes you to Key West on a beautiful afternoon like this, Charlie John?"

"I'm going on a treasure hunt."

***

Jack was back on his porch, leaning over his guitar, writing lyrics and notes on a yellow pad perched on his knees. Packing for his trip to Wilmington in a few days was the furthest thing from his mind since he was busy writing his first hit single. The fact that he wasn't a very good guitar player and that the thought of singing in front of a crowd terrified him hadn't crossed his mind. He wrote, he played, he scratched out words, he started over a couple of times, but he was solely focused on getting the song down on paper.

After a couple of hours and a couple of beers, he finished writing his first tune. He looked up from his notes as if expecting a nonjudgmental audience to have magically appeared on his front lawn. The only souls in sight were Stevie, the bratty kid from next door, and the grey cat from down the block that hung out under his porch. Stevie caught his look and flipped him off before running into his house.

Jack performed the first song he had ever written to a cat whose name he didn't know.

***

After a little bite at Bobalu's on Big Coppitt Key, which was at Charlie's request but somehow she paid for, they drove the last four miles to Key West. Mary Jane's arrival wasn't exactly what she had imagined. She rode into town with the top down, an old bicycle sticking up from the backseat, and a stew bum cowboy who smelled of sweat, cigarettes, and beer sitting next to her.

When she dropped him at Smathers Beach, he gave her an appreciative nod and a snort that she took as a "thank you," then he mounted his bike and rode away. As he disappeared in her rearview mirror, she had to admit that in their short time together, she had kind of liked the guy. She wondered if she would ever run into him again.

Charlie had suggested a cheap but clean place to stay, the Sea Shell Motel on South Street. She found it quickly, and for twenty-eight dollars per night, she had a bunk bed in the female dorm room of the hostel. Using Charlie's name, or John as the woman behind the desk knew him, didn't seem to garner her any special treatment as he had promised. It was a bed, a place to lay her head for a few nights.

Mary Jane returned to her car and tried to raise the top in case it rained. The top mechanism jammed halfway up, but with a little pushing, she was able to get it to go back down. She needed a drink and it was nearly sunset. She asked a passing couple which way it was to Mallory Square, and based solely on the direction they pointed, she set off to see what Key West was all about.

***

It was a twelve-hour drive from St. Simons Island to Wilmington, Delaware, including a few gas stops and one fifteen-minute nap at a rest area outside of Richmond. Jack had packed what he needed into his Jeep, made a trip to the Goodwill, filled two garbage cans, and stored the remainder of his worldly possessions in the back of his friend's garage.

In Wilmington, he followed the directions to a condo the company had rented for him until he found permanent housing. As promised, the door was unlocked. The small condo was modestly but adequately furnished, the refrigerator was stocked with a few necessities, including a six-pack of Pale Ale from Crooked Hammock Brewing. On the counter, next to a fruit basket with a "Welcome" banner, was a set of keys and a garage door opener. Jack popped open a beer and walked back outside, where he punched the button on the opener and watched the second door in the long line of garage doors open to an empty single car unit. "Cool," he said to himself.

CHAPTER FOUR

Some Big Time Buccaneers

The Green Parrot was more of a local dive than a tourist bar. It sat a few blocks off Duval but still managed to attract a fair number of visitors, drawn in by cheaper drinks and a seedier crowd. The place was quiet, even for a Sunday night. A few regulars hung out at the bar and a couple of tourists loitered at the tables up front.

Charlie took his stool in the back corner behind the pool table and slowly drank his beer. For three nights, he had patiently sat in the bar waiting for a guy to show up. Both Friday and Saturday nights, he had suffered through some really bad cover bands, so he was relieved that the Parrot's stereo was now playing a variety of classic rock.

He recognized them the moment they walked in the bar even though he'd never met them. Angel, the ring leader, was Puerto Rican, maybe Cuban. He was the shortest of the three men, better dressed than the other two, wearing a Guayabera shirt, slacks, and a Tommy Bahama style hat. He may have been the shortest of the bunch, but it was immediately clear that he was the leader by the way the other two men interacted with him.

Beside him, looking over the room with a watchful eye, was a large, dark-complexioned man who was clearly his muscle. Muscle was a term that might have fit the man years ago. Now he was just fat. He was probably a mean son-of-a-bitch, Charlie thought, certainly armed and willing to quickly protect his boss, but while he looked tough, his days as an effective street fighter were long gone. The third man was white. He was the nervous type; his eyes shifted around the room quickly. He was in the wrong line of work. Charlie quickly identified him as the business guy, the accountant. In a fight, he'd be the first guy out the door.

They took a table towards the front of the bar and ordered drinks. After the waitress set the drinks on the table, Angel took a few sips before shifting his chair to look around the bar. That was when he and Charlie made eye contact. Charlie gave him a nod and tipped his beer slightly to the man. Angel had no reaction; he turned back towards his two companions. A few minutes later, the muscle got up and slowly wandered back towards Charlie.

"Are you John?" he asked in a casual voice as beads of sweat rolled down his face.

"Yeah," replied Charlie.

The man put his hand on the bulge near his waistline, asking, "Are you packing?" clearly indicating that he was.

Charlie took a sip of his beer before saying, "No."

"Angel would like to talk to you," he said as he pointed his thumb towards the front of the bar.

***

The knock at the door startled him. He had done a half-assed job of unpacking and hung a few things up so he had something to wear to work that wasn't too wrinkled, then sat down in front of some mindless TV show to finish off the six-pack from the fridge. He opened the door and there stood Ed Baxter, a big, loud, smiley fella, the Managing Director of his company.

"Jack, you old bastard!" he said while over enthusiastically shaking his hand. "Welcome to Wilmington. How the hell was the drive?"

Ed bulldozed his way into the door past Jack, smiling and laughing and carrying on about how glad he was that Jack was joining them at the home office. Jack had only met Ed on two occasions: once at a meeting when they were trying to get a contract with the Department of Defense and another time when he had visited the St. Simons office. Ed acted like they were long lost friends.

Everything about Ed was big. He was a big man, he had a big house, a big Mercedes, he was the loudest guy in the room, the biggest personality, the biggest spender. Ed was just big. He talked like he was from Jersey, only louder. Along with his late partner, Bill Hutton, he had built a medium-sized engineering firm through hard work, long hours, and gutsy decisions.

After Bill Hutton died of a stroke at his desk, Ed had decided to live what was left of his life to the fullest, which to him meant spending as much of his money as he could, living large and loud. He loved expensive cars, jewelry, wine, and women.

Ed still kept his hands in the firm; he saw himself as the rainmaker, the big dog with the connections. He was certain his firm couldn't survive without him. The general consensus around the company, however, was that Baxter and Hutton had become successful because of Ed Baxter and now somehow continued to thrive despite him.

"Is this the place Arlene found you? What a shit hole. We'll get you something better in a week or so."

"It's fine," Jack started to say, but Ed cut him off.

"What do you have to drink around here?" he asked.

"I have a beer, but that's about it."

"Beer? We can do better than that," said Ed with smile. "Let's go over to the club and have a few cocktails." He glanced at the gaudy Rolex. "Ah shit, they'll be closed by now. That's the only problem with Wilmington on a Sunday night is the whole damn town closes early. You can't find a decent drink after nine. No matter, we'll have lots of time to drink and get acquainted.

"Hey, the reason I came over here was I wanted to tell you that all the upper management is going down to Captiva Island tomorrow for a meeting and I want you to go along. I know you just got here from down there, but what the hell, let's go back."

Jack didn't know exactly what to say. He had expected to go to the office in the morning, meet lots of new people, set up his desk, find the bathroom, the coffee pot, and supply closet, and now his boss' boss was asking him to go to Captiva. He had heard stories about the legendary managers' trips to Captiva. "Okay, if that's what you need me to do."

"Great! We've chartered a plane. You'll need to be at the executive terminal at the airport by eight tomorrow morning. Glad you're going along! Geez, I guess I'd better get home and pack so I don't have to spend the entire trip parading around in my Speedo!" he said with a big, loud laugh.

Jack closed the door after Ed and shook his head while asking himself, What the hell just happened?

***

There were no formal introductions in a meeting like this. Angel nonchalantly nodded towards the chair across from him and Charlie sat down. The muscle stood behind Charlie, casually leaning against the wall but ready to strike if a threat appeared.

Angel looked at the unimpressive figure across the table from him, noting the long hair, scraggly beard, and dirty cowboy hat. "I'm told you may be able to help me with a distribution problem I have here," said the smuggler after a moment.

Charlie didn't want to sound overly enthusiastic. He thought playing a bit cool would be the right move. "I can sell a lot of product if I'm properly motivated. Are you able to supply enough to keep the lower Keys happy?"

The muscle behind him laughed. Angel shot his man an angry look before saying, "I can supply enough to keep Southern Florida happy. And if I was 'properly motivated,' I could come up with enough to keep the southern half of the United States happy."

Looking into his eyes, Charlie was unable to tell if the man was lying or not. The amount of marijuana he was talking about was staggering. Charlie was clearly out of his league.

For years, he had sold pot out of his little business on the beach, a quarter ounce or a joint at a time, to help supplement his raft rental income. The supply dried up when his source had suddenly disappeared. Looking to finally strike it rich, Charlie had made some inquiries with a few guys he knew, and after a week or so, heard that the off-shore supplier wanted to meet with him. If he could put this deal together, he would be rich beyond his wildest dreams.

"So, tell me," Angel said after taking a drink, "how is a little piss ant beach dealer on a bicycle going to distribute the amount that I need to move here?"

Charlie leaned forward, putting his elbows on the table. "Your last distributor drew heat from the cops, the DEA, even your competition because everybody knew what he was and what he did. Shit, driving around in that pimped-out car like he owned the place, what an ass. Nobody pays attention to a little piss ant beach dealer, even you. If you think that's what I'm about, you've misunderstood. It's not a game, boy. It's life."

Angel clearly bought it. He leaned back and took another sip of his drink, never taking his eyes off the man across from him. "I suggest we start small, a couple of kilos. Show me how quickly you can move that and we'll talk about growing your business." Angel looked at Charlie silently for several moments before asking, "Are you an honest man?"

The question was so far out in left field, given the business they were discussing, that Charlie wasn't sure how to answer. He replied, "Yes, yes, I am."

Angel stood up to leave. "There's no room for an honest man in this greedy town." Then he turned and walked out of the bar.

Charlie swallowed hard. Just like that, he was a big-time drug dealer.

***

The two-and-a-half-hour flight from Wilmington to Fort Myers, Florida aboard the chartered Hawker 800, Jack's first on a private jet, was pleasant enough. Ed started drinking as soon as he got on board and the other executives seemed to know the drill. Join in or face certain scrutiny. Ed told jokes the entire way, laughing loudly at his own antics. Jack even found some of them funny after his third Bloody Mary.

It was an hour's ride From Fort Myers to the South Sea Island Resort on Captiva Island. The only formal plan the first evening was dinner. Ed slapped Jack on the back and said, "Go have fun. Enjoy yourself. We'll see you at dinner. We don't get too much done on these trips."

With that, Jack called his old high school buddy, Randy White, who lived across the sound on Pine Island. Randy was just getting ready to head out fishing and told Jack to meet him at the dock in thirty minutes. Jack smiled. So far, his new position wasn't working out too bad. His first day he got buzzed with the boss on a private jet, he checked into a tropical resort, and was about to go fishing with an old friend. If the first day on his new job was any indication, the move to Wilmington just might work out.

Jack was thrilled to be back on Charlotte Harbor. His great-uncle had lived in the tiny town of El Jobean and Jack and his father made several trips down to go fishing with him when he was younger. After his uncle had died, Jack and his father quit making the trips, but he always remembered them. Those memories and this area held a special place in his heart.

***

The trip to Captiva wasn't as non-business as Ed had led Jack to believe. While Jack was walking to the dock to meet Randy, the top executives were gathering in Ed's room. They had a big problem up in North Dakota and had to figure out a way they could talk Jack, a talented engineer but certifiable southern beach boy, into moving from St. Simons to Wilmington to Minot, North Dakota.

Ed was convinced that some wining and dining, a hot woman on his lap, and a modest raise would do the trick. Marco Begovich, his manager on St. Simons, wasn't as certain. "It took a lot of convincing to get him to move up to Wilmington. Asking him to move to Minot could put him over the edge."

Ed rolled his eyes. "Your problem, Marco, is that you're a bad judge of character. The boy was elated that I asked him down here. He feels like he's part of the team, part of the big picture. Nancy will be down here Wednesday morning. I'll ask her to cuddle up to him, we'll feed him a nice dinner, get him drunk on some good wine, tell him how important he is to all of us, and convince him that Minot is a short-term deal. He'll go up there for us and the problem with Nuverra will be solved in a few months."

Ralph Lindsay spoke up first. "The immediate problems with the Nuverra contract is fixable, but the long-term issue is Lead Engineer turnover. I'm not sure your surfer boy is the right move. If we can't keep him up there for two or three years, Nuverra's going to dump us. They've made that very clear." He paused for a moment, thinking his next words through before saying them. "Ed, I'm not sure your girlfriend in a tight dress, kissing him on the ear while getting him drunk, is going to convince him to save our butts up north."

"Don't worry," said Ed with a wave of his hand. "We'll let the boy play for a day or two, stroke his ego, and tell him how important he is to our success. Nancy flirting with him won't hurt. I can read this kid like a book. I've got this handled."

***

After a great day of fishing around Pine Island Sound on his friend Randy's flatboat, Jack was treated to an incredible dinner with the company's top executives and managers. Ed ordered several very expensive bottles of wine and made certain to keep Jack's glass full. It was obvious they were all cuddling up to him for some reason, and while he was both curious and suspicious, he was also smart enough to play along and take advantage of the golden boy treatment. When they mentioned that they had a couple of consultants coming in to meet with them on Tuesday, Jack asked what time they were scheduled to meet, since Randy had invited him to go sailing.

"You go have fun, Jack," said Ed in a booming voice. "We'll handle the consultants. Those overpaid bastards have their noses crammed so far up my ass that they can't seem to see the problem to begin with. Maybe we can have them do a quick rundown at dinner tomorrow night."

Jack smiled, he didn't know what had changed or what the corporate boys were up to, but he was going to play it for all it was worth. If the boss said to go sailing, then by damn, he was going sailing. So, on Tuesday, they went sailing and found some great wind!

***

The first big drug deal of his new career seemed to go incredibly smooth. The fat guy, Angel's bodyguard, delivered four pounds of Columbian Gold. Charlie paid for it by draining the money he had saved in his old cigar box. He spread the word to a few guys that he knew as dealers on the island. With almost no supply available, he was able to sell his entire inventory in a little over an hour and they were clamoring for more. At a 100% markup, Charlie was excited to get his hands on more. The money was easy.

***

After a great day of sailing on Tuesday, Jack met Ed for dinner, just the two of them. Ed promised him the "best damn steak on this island" over at Doc Fords.

"Jack, I haven't been honest with you," said Ed after a couple of cocktails. "I brought you down here for a reason. We're in trouble and we need your help."

"How can I help?" asked Jack.

"Have you looked around the company? We're all a bunch of old men running the show," Ed said with a slow shake of his head. "I got so busy building the company that I forgot to hire young talented guys like you. In a few years, we're all going to retire and the company is screwed. We want to fast track you to the top, because we need new blood: young, energetic guys who can keep Baxter and Hutton growing long after we're gone. When we were looking at who we had, your name was at the top of the list and I agreed. You're the type of guy who can guarantee success after all of us old duffers retire. What do ya say?"

Jack was flattered. They thought enough about him to bring him along on the management retreat and they believed he could run the company. Ed was telling him he was being promoted up the chain quickly, heading from computer design to management. "I don't know what to say, sir. I'm thrilled you think so much of me. I hope I can meet your expectations."

Ed waved to the waitress to bring another round of drinks. "All you need to do is follow my lead, help me out, and I can promise you a partnership in less than ten years. How does that sound?" Ed could tell from the look on Jack's face that he had him.

"By the way," Ed said with a grin, "we're all getting together Friday morning. I'll be handing out the annual bonus checks and I know there's one for you. That's a meeting you don't want to miss." Jack looked appropriately surprised. Ed sat back and finished his cocktail in one swallow. He was good.

***

Angel made the second drop himself, ten pounds of pot. The fat guy stood near the car in the parking lot, ever vigilant with a mean look about him. Charlie was a little short of cash to pay for the extra couple of pounds, but Angel allowed him to owe it to him. Charlie sold six pounds before dark. When he arrived at Smathers Beach the next morning, two of his dealers were waiting to buy the remaining stock. They both dickered the price up until one guy had to drop out. Charlie went across the road to the pay phone and left a message on Angel's machine. "I need twenty." Business was good.

***

Ed met Nancy's flight and gave her a hug and a kiss. It was ten in the morning and he was already sweaty, she thought. She was still secretly angry with him that he had bumped her off the chartered jet at the last moment to make room for some other guy. She couldn't get a commercial flight for two days. But she gave him a smile and a kiss and played the part.

Theirs was a financial relationship, and while it was unspoken, they both knew it. Nancy was more than thirty years his junior, and she was a beautiful woman by any standard. She could have almost any man, but she didn't want any man; she wanted a rich man. Her close friends understood, others harshly judged her, but she didn't care.

Nancy had never been in love. She told people that she had been born without the love gene. She didn't understand the emotion or the passion that others seemed to feel and express so quickly and openly. People had committed murder over love, they had committed suicide over love. Nancy didn't get it. She lived in a world filled with an emotion she didn't understand and with people in relationships she couldn't relate to.

But she did understand money and she knew she liked it. To her, a relationship with Ed was like a high paying job that she didn't like very much. Her "career goal" was to get him to marry her, which would solidify her future. He would either eventually divorce her or die. In a divorce, she would end up with a bucket of money. If she hung around until he died, she would probably end up with it all. Ed had been married twice before. He had three kids from his first marriage, all who hated him.

***

Jack had never been much of a golfer but accepted the invitation to play nine holes on Wednesday morning with a couple of the company execs, D.H. Moss and Jock Hewett. A beer on the first hole took care of his hangover, and by the third hole, he was feeling and playing pretty well and actually having fun.

***

"Nancy doll, I need you to do me a big favor," Ed said once they got settled in the backseat of the car service's Escalade.

"Sure, what do you need?" she asked as if she was game for anything.

Ed turned towards her and took on a serious look. "We've got a big problem up in North Dakota. I've got the guy out here on the island that I think can solve it for us, but the fellas don't think he'll take the assignment. I've been stroking his ego and filling him with good wine, but I need your help to put him over the top. Could you snuggle up to him, make him feel good about himself? I'll tell him you're my niece or something like that."

Nancy didn't like the feeling of the request at all. She wasn't a call girl or Ed's little harlot. If she agreed to this, could she become a pawn in future contract negotiations too? "Ed, honey, I don't like the idea of cuddling up with some other guy. You know you're my one and only," she lied.

"I know that, sugar. But we really need this guy to go up there and help solve this problem. I wouldn't ask, but there's millions at stake."

Nancy played it, since there were millions involved. Maybe this was the bargaining chip that would get a ring on her finger. She sat back in her seat and looked out the window. "Ugh, what's this guy look like?"

"He's young, twenty-five or twenty-six, looks of a handsome movie star, a body that's just insane, kind of a southern surfer type. What do ya say?"

She was intrigued. Being from New Orleans herself, she always had a soft spot for those southern boys with that certain accent. Did Ed say "young"? That could be a pleasant change from her overweight, sweaty, and loud boyfriend. "Just how 'cuddly' do you want me to get?" she asked.

Ed smiled. "Show him a good time, but don't forget that you're my doll and when the week is up, you and me are going back to the way it's always been."

"You're going to owe me big for this, Eddie Boy."

"You know I'll take good care of you. I always do," he said while leaning over for another kiss.

***

Twenty pounds of pot, on top of what he had sold over the previous eighteen hours, proved to be the tipping point on the supply and demand curve for Key West. Eager to sell his inventory, Charlie borrowed a beat-up pickup from a friend and drove up to Big Pine Key, where he sold the entire remaining stash to one dealer. From the Winn-Dixie on Big Pine, he left another message on Angel's machine asking for another twenty pounds. The Key West supply would dry up in a few days, but in the meantime, he could sell another ten on Big Pine and probably the rest on Marathon Key.

His little business was thriving and it seemed that he could sell everything he could get his hands on if he was willing to drive a few hours. He thought he might have to get his own car, maybe even a driver's license. Hell, he thought, maybe he would just hire a driver and sit in the backseat. He smiled as he drove back towards Key West. It seemed that Charlie had finally found his gold.

CHAPTER FIVE

Nancy, The Sensual Kind...

After playing nine holes with the guys, they had lunch in the clubhouse. Jack had enjoyed himself, but the last couple of nights were catching up with him. He walked back to his room, casually observing all the flora and fauna at the tropical resort. It really was a nice place. After a shower and a nap, he was ready for a drink at the bar. If he charged it to the room, it was free to him.

Her looks reminded him of an exotic sports car, lean and sleek and sexy as hell. She sat alone at the bar, sipping on a martini and looking bored. She wasn't dressed unusually sexy—a pair of navy shorts that fit very well and a white tank top—but she radiated sexuality, beauty, and class. The very least he could do was to sidle up next to her and strike up a conversation, at least until her husband or boyfriend showed up to chase him off.

Making eye contact with the bartender, he ordered a Myer's Rum and tonic. He turned to her and pointed at her drink, asking, "Can I get you another?"

She smiled. Despite all of her other prominent features, her smile was one of her most valuable assets. "Well, thank you. That's very kind of you." She held out her hand. "I'm Nancy."

Jack about fell over his tongue when he caught her smile, her southern accent, and her natural beauty. "I'm Jack, my pleasure. Are you saving this stool for your husband?" He was sure she would brush him off. He hoped she wouldn't call security or pull out her mace.

She blushed slightly, a blush she had practiced a hundred times in the mirror. "I'm not married. My uncle might come down after a bit, but you're welcome to join me. Are you from around here?"

There was something about the way she talked, her Louisiana accent, the way she moved her head, the right inflection of speech and tilt at exactly the right time. Her smile was beyond sexy; she was the sensual kind, wild-eyed and beautiful. She was captivating and Jack was immediately in lust. Even more surprising to Jack was that she seemed to really be interested in him.

"You're an engineer?" she said with a bit of surprise after he mentioned it. "You might know my uncle, Ed Baxter? He's down here for a bunch of meetings."

Jack laughed. "Ed's my boss! We had dinner together last night." He should have been wondering if hitting on Ed's niece would end his career, but he was far too excited to care.

She laughed at every joke and appeared captivated by his stories. After a second drink, she paused for a moment and gave him a thoughtful look before saying, "Let's get out of here." Jack quickly agreed. He was leaving the bar with one of the most beautiful and captivating women he had ever seen. Why wouldn't he agree?

They walked to the dock where they were told that they couldn't join the sunset cruise because they hadn't made reservations, but a hundred-dollar bill solved the problem. They enjoyed the sunset and another cocktail as they sat very close to each other. Nancy listened to him intently and gave him the right smile and a little nudge or a touch of his hand at just the right time.

She perfectly performed her part in an unnamed melodrama, a part she had played many times before. Jack was smitten, still amazed that such a woman would be so immediately interested in him. He was undoubtedly in for the ride.

After the cruise, they walked to The Green Flash where they shared an order of Oysters Rockefeller, then split the Surf and Turf special while gazing across the table at each other in the glow of the candlelight. In the moonlight, they strolled up the beach with no destination in mind. After a bit, Nancy reached over and took his hand. They walked in silence for quite a while, hand in hand, enjoying the breeze from the ocean and enjoying each other's touch.

Nancy looked over at him as they walked. He wasn't the type of man she had ever pursued. He wasn't wealthy or egotistical. He was probably a few years younger than she, he was polite, honest, and she immediately had picked up on a sense of innocence about him. She liked Jack, she was enjoying their evening, and she realized it was the first time in a long time that she could admit to herself that she was having fun.

After a while, they stopped along the beach and looked out at the moon. Jack turned towards her and took both her hands, then looked into her eyes and gave her a kiss—not a long or passionate or wildly sexual one, but a nice, innocent kiss. It was a kiss unlike any she had received since high school, maybe even junior high. She felt a strange twinge in the pit of her stomach.

Back at the resort, Jack politely offered to walk her to her room. She declined because she didn't want an awkward scene to develop; her room was Ed's room. Jack asked her if he could kiss her goodnight, and in the breezeway, they shared their second kiss, longer than the first, but still very sweet and innocent.

She walked to Ed's room with a smile on her face and the strangest feeling about her. Her smile went away when she opened the door and heard him snoring. At least he wasn't awake. She'd take his snoring over his drunken love making anytime.

Jack crawled into his bed thinking about Nancy, wondering about the morning and brooding about how she might act towards him in the daylight. He fell asleep thinking of her amazing smile.

Nancy lay in bed next to Ed, who was snoring like a chainsaw. She tried to recall the last time she had been excited to be with a man, the last time she had felt such sweet innocence, such sincerity and honesty in another human.

As Ed stirred, she remembered the first time she saw him in the bar at the Ritz-Carlton in New Orleans. A group of five men sat at a table laughing, toasting, and bragging about all the money they were going to make on some condo development they were building on the Louisiana shore. He caught her eye and was soon at the bar next to her, buying her glasses of the most expensive champagne available. Soon they were dancing, and by the end of the night, after hearing that he was flying back to Delaware on a private jet, she was sleeping with him. They kept in touch for a few weeks before he invited her to a big party he was throwing at his vacation home on Cape May, which she accepted.

Her father always said guys like this had the long money. They were guys who had the money and could spend it all, and they were ready to stay in the game until the rest were gone. Nancy had arrived to the party fashionably late, dressed to the nines. The guests were all the beautiful people—doctors and lawyers and assorted ego-maniacs. They were the type of people who liked living life to the extreme, like the fat cardiologist that looked like he was a cheesecake away from a heart attack. The ladies were all scantily dressed and surgically blessed. It was her kind of crowd.

When she walked into the party looking like a self-absorbed movie star, heads turned in her direction. A great little band named the Bamboo's or something like that played near the pool, but nobody seemed to pay much attention to them. It didn't take Ed more than a few minutes to find her. He made it clear that she was indeed his very special guest. He said, "Tell me what you need, and anything you ask for gets an automatic yes."

They visited long enough to make the rounds, so Ed could show off his date from New Orleans to all of his friends. Then he took her by the arm and said, "You must see my place. And I must tell you, that dress would look good lying crumpled on my bedroom floor."

Nancy gave him a well-rehearsed laugh at the ancient line as they strolled across the lawn that was littered with bottles of bourbon and vodka and gin. As they retired inside, the band played on. Two week later, she moved from her second-floor apartment in New Orleans to a two-story mansion overlooking the Delaware River.

Nancy hadn't ever questioned her relationship with Ed; it was a means to an end, a retirement plan. Her father had been a disciple of Zig Zigler and had always quoted his line, "You can have anything you want if you just help enough people get what they want." She was sure this wasn't exactly what he had meant, but it had long been her justification.

As she fell asleep, she wondered what her life with a middle-income, twenty-something mechanical engineer would be like.

***

Jack woke up early and went for a run. After a shower, he went to the restaurant near the pool for breakfast. Not finding her, he ate alone, then slowly read the paper next to the pool. He couldn't concentrate on the articles because he was too busy watching for her.

***

"Wake up, sleepy head," said Ed as he shook her. He was showered and dressed in a horrible tropical shirt and wearing an awful aftershave again. "How did last night go?"

She stretched for a moment and then through a yawn said, "He's a really nice guy. He said he was very excited to be working with you in Wilmington and thought he could learn a lot from you. I think he's a pretty solid company man."

"That's good news. Listen, I want you to spend the day with him and keep his ego bursting because tomorrow I'm going to spring the North Dakota transfer on him. Can you do that for me, sweetie?"

Nancy was a pro; she stuck out her lower lip just a bit. "But I came down here to spend time with you, babe."

"I know you did," said Ed, "and I'm going to make it up to you. How about we fly down to the Bahamas in a few weeks, just you and me?"

Spending the day flirting with a cute guy, a trip to the Bahamas, and another step towards her big goal? How could she say no? But she played it for all it was worth. "Okay, but you're going to owe me big, and I mean really big."

***

It was just before eleven when Nancy snuck up behind Jack. She softly put her hands over his eyes and whispered in his ear, "Promise me you'll say yes to whatever question I ask next."

Jack felt her velvety hands on his face. He could smell her intoxicating perfume and felt her breath on his ear. "Yes!" he answered instantly.

"Spend the day with me," she whispered. "Let's get a car and go for a drive, maybe find an empty beach somewhere for a picnic and a swim. Let's just go be alone somewhere."

Jack could feel the blood suddenly pulsating through his entire body. "Yes!" he quickly answered.

***

Charlie started the fourth full day of his drug dealing business with more money in his pocket than he had ever held. An old acquaintance had driven down from Key Largo to find him, saying that he could sell everything Charlie could get his hands on. Angel and the fat man met him behind the Monroe County Tax Collector's Office, a building that also held the Driver's License office, with a couple of duffle bags full of weed. With an advance from his Key Largo buddy, Charlie paid for the new shipment in full.

"I keep finding more sources to sell to. Do you really have enough to keep up?" he asked.

Angel smiled, his gold-lined teeth shining in the sun. "You keep coming with the cash, I'll keep supplying the gold." That was all he had to hear. Charlie smiled back and turned away without a comment.

***

Jack rushed back to his room to get ready for what promised to be one of the best days of his life. He called his buddy Randy to ask where was the best and most private beach in the area because he had a hot date...and he meant hot!

Randy could hear the excitement in his old friend's voice. "Tell you what, if you can cool your jets for about forty-five minutes, I'll meet you at the dock with my boat, a big beach blanket, and a cooler full of ice. You go to the store, get a bottle of wine and a picnic lunch. Drop me back on Pine Island and then I'll tell you where to find the most romantic and secluded beach on Cayo Costa."

Nancy met Jack back near the pool. She wore a yellow string bikini that was easily visible through a patterned sheer coverup. She had a little beach bag over her shoulder and was sporting a floppy beach hat that covered her now braided hair. They had fun shopping, flirting, and laughing while they perused the tiny grocery store for cheese and crackers, a homemade loaf of

French bread, some fun spreads, and a couple of bottles of wine. Randy was waiting at the dock when they arrived. He helped Nancy into the boat, and when she turned her head, he looked at Jack and silently said, "Wow!"

After dropping Randy back on Pine Island, Jack raced for Cayo Costa and the little beach tucked around Pejuan Point. Nancy snuggled close to him and by the time the island came into sight, Jack didn't care which beach they found. He dropped the anchor in two feet of water and hopped over the side. Jack offered her a hand and she made a good show of slipping off the boat and right into his arms, sliding her body down his and kissing him as her feet hit the sandy bottom.

As the afternoon flew by, they swam, they drank wine, they spread the blanket in the shade of a couple of palms. Nancy laid her head on Jack's chest as he enjoyed a short, wine-infused nap. They talked about his life on St. Simons and her life in New Orleans. She discreetly left out the past year that she had lived in Wilmington and wondered how that was going to play out when Jack eventually found out she was Ed's girlfriend, not his niece. She had lived so many lies over the last several years that it shouldn't have bothered her, but this time it did.

When the sun dropped over the trees on the island, they loaded up the boat and drove out on Pine Island Sound to watch the sunset. They made out like teenagers as the sun sank low on the horizon. When it was gone, it set the sky ablaze. Jack looked out at the amazing spectacle unfolding before them and said in quiet admiration, "The world's biggest canvas gets painted every day."

As they started back for Pine Island, she kissed him on the cheek and used a line she had said many times before. "I don't want this day to end because you've been a part of it." After she said it, her breath seemed to be sucked out of her chest as she realized it was the first time she had ever meant it.

They tied up in Randy's slip after dark and walked hand in hand two blocks to his house. He gave them a ride back to Captiva. He couldn't help but notice the growing affection between them. He was jealous. It had been years since any woman had looked at him like that.

Back at the resort, Jack suggested they shower, then meet for dinner at the restaurant just off the lobby. As they walked past, Nancy heard Ed's boisterous laughter coming from inside. "I have a better idea," she said with a smile. "I'll run to my room, grab some clothes, then I can shower in your room while we wait for room service."

Jack readily agreed. "That's a much better idea!"

They showered together, and after a few hours of love making, Jack called for room service just minutes before the kitchen closed. They shared dinner naked on the bed, then fell asleep, and thanks to Jack's forethought in turning the air conditioner all the way down, they cuddled all night.

Jack tiptoed out of the room early and went for one of the best runs of his life. He floated above the beach and hardly noticed the incredible morning on the Gulf Coast. There was snook in the surf and the pelicans were crashing on bait. The wind was cool coming off the ocean, but he didn't notice. His mind was on the beautiful and vibrant woman back in his bed.

As he ran, he thought about his time on Captiva. On Monday, he went fishing with a good friend. On Tuesday, they went sailing, they found some great wind. On Wednesday, he met her, so Thursday was just a blur. He finally stopped and took a breather, then turned around and ran back to the south. He hadn't made a single meeting, and he barely used his room. He smelled a little like Captain Morgan's and her perfume. When they handed out the bonus money later this morning, he'd stop by and say hello, but he wouldn't stay too long. He had places he needed to go. He made a mental note to remember to write some of those lines down.

He stopped by the restaurant on his way back to the room and ordered breakfast and mimosas for two. Nancy was still sleeping when he snuck back in, so he stepped into the shower and was just pulling on a pair of shorts when breakfast arrived.

"Wow," she said as she stretched awake. "Look at you, showered, shaved, and you cooked breakfast," she said with a wonderful smile.

Jack handed her a mimosa and sat on the bed next to her. "I have a meeting with Ed in about twenty minutes," he said with a frown.

She touched his arm. "Jack, I won't be here when you get back. I was going to tell you yesterday that my flight was this morning, but I didn't want to ruin our perfect day."

"When can we see each other again?" he asked. "I'd love to fly down to New Orleans, or you can always come up to Wilmington."

The gravity of what she had done was starting to sink in, especially as she looked into his innocent eyes and heard the sincerity in his voice. There was no way she could back out now; she had run out of lies and eventually he would find out the truth. He'd be crushed.

She did the only thing she knew to distract a man at a time like this, she drank her mimosa in two big gulps, then grabbed him behind the neck and pulled her to him, saying, "You're going to be late for your meeting."

CHAPTER SIX

We've Got This Problem Up In North Dakota

"Jack!" yelled Ed from across the room in a booming but happy voice. He held a Bloody Mary in his hand, his arm around the Pittsburgh office manager. "Where in the heck have you been?" As he walked closer, Ed could see his wrinkled shirt and his slightly messed-up hair. "Ah, haa-haa! I haven't seen you or my niece in days! I know where you've been, you dog!"

Jack caught two of the execs in the room shoot each other a strange glance at the mention of Ed's "niece." "Sorry I'm late," he said as Ed handed him a fresh Bloody Mary.

"No worries," Ed said in his big, loud voice. He reached into his pocket and pulled out an envelope. "I've got something for you. It's not much, but it's not a bad bonus for a guy who's only been on the executive team for a week. Let's grab a table in the shade. I've got something else to talk to you about."

It was the first Jack had heard about being on the executive team. As he followed Ed out towards the pool, he peeked inside the envelope. There was a check made out to him for $5,400.00, more than a month's pay. He tucked it into his pocket before they made it to the table.

Sitting down, Ed took a sip of his drink. "Jack, have you had a good time down here?"

"It's been a great time," he said honestly.

"I understand you and Nancy are kind of a thing," he said with a wink and a smile.

"She's been a lot of fun to hang out with," he said, not wanting to tell Uncle Ed too much.

He smiled. "I'll bet she's been fun! Hey, listen, we've got a problem that's come up and we think you can solve it for us. As a member of the executive team, we sometimes need our boys to step up and go the extra mile."

Jack smiled. "You've certainly been good to me. How can I help you?"

Ed slapped him on the back. "Glad to hear it. I knew you'd be willing to help us. We have a client called Nuverra. They're a big environmental company up in North Dakota, and we have a multi-million-dollar contract with them. It's been very lucrative for us. We had a guy running the office up there, Jeff Park. Park and his boys screwed up on a big project, had the numbers all fucked up and cost us a lot of money. When I jumped his ass about it, he up and quit."

Jack hadn't heard much after the words "North Dakota." "What do you need from me?" he asked with some apprehension.

Ed leaned forward, placing his elbows on the table. "Jack, I need you to go up there and fix this. They need a guy who is smart enough to fix the screw-up, and they need somebody who can show them that we have some stability in our leadership. Can you do that for us?"

The summers in North Dakota probably weren't too bad, Jack thought. It might be fun to see that part of the country for a few months. "How long do you think you need me up there?" he asked.

"Not long, just a couple, three-four years," said Ed. Jack looked for the grin on Ed's face indicating he was joking, but he didn't see it.

***

Jack walked back to his room feeling betrayed, broken, and lost. He opened the door to find her gone, everything except her scent. He had asked Ed if he could think about the North Dakota transfer over the weekend and get back to him on Monday. Ed seemed shocked that he didn't want to jump on the position but said to call him at the Pittsburgh office on Monday morning.

When he got up to leave the table, Ed turned and said, "Oh, by the way, the jet is full on the way back. You'll have to fly commercial and expense it."

Jack guessed that he would be flying home on the jet with the boys if he had accepted the job up north. Ed's message was loud and clear. Take the transfer or plan to be treated like shit.

Jack had had enough of Captiva. He was ready to get back home, or at least back to Wilmington. He called the front desk and asked them to get him a cab to the airport, then tossed his clothes in his bag, not bothering to fold any of them. In his haste to get packed, he almost missed the note from Nancy.

Jack,

I had a truly wonderful time with you. Honestly, yesterday was one of the best days of my life. I'll call you soon, I promise. Be careful. Ed may be playing you.

Kisses,

Nancy

A brief thought crossed his mind: he wasn't too far behind her. Maybe he would see her at the airport. He rushed out of the room, into the waiting cab, and asked the driver to get him there as fast as he could.

At the airport, Jack purchased a one-way ticket for Wilmington. Once through security, he desperately searched the terminal for any flight that was heading anywhere in the general direction of New Orleans. As he finally boarded his flight, he stopped at the door of the jetway and took one last look across the concourse, hoping against hope to see her face. He turned and walked down the jetway.

***

Had Nancy gone back to Wilmington, they would have likely been on the same flight. Instead, she had decided to fly to Miami, where she would spend a few days with her closest real friend, Samantha.

They had both attended Loyola, but Sam had actually graduated and had a good job as an events coordinator for the City of Miami. When Nancy called, asking if she could spend the weekend, Sam gave a little squeal of excitement. It had been more than a year since they had spent time together, about the same time Nancy had moved to Delaware to live with the rich pig.

Sam met her at the airport curb in her little Miata convertible. As they stuffed her luggage in the tiny trunk, Sam told her that her boyfriend was out of town all week and it was going to be a ladies' weekend. She had big plans that started with a pedicure and wine at her favorite spa. It only took her a few minutes to realize that something was wrong. Nancy wasn't being herself.

***

Jack had three drinks on the flight to Newark, two while he waited for the flight to Wilmington, and two on that flight. He was hurtling through space, in a cramped metal tube with a bunch of screaming kids, and really small bags of peanuts. Flying commercial wasn't fun. He had decided the solution was to self-medicate. Jack laughed when he noticed a man on his last flight wearing a t-shirt that said, "Booze is the Duct Tape of Life."

By the time he arrived in Delaware, he was boiled. His Jeep was parked on the far side of the airport. He hopped into a cab and asked the driver to take him to the Executive Terminal but changed his mind and asked him to take him home instead. He knew better than to drive.

After struggling with the front door of the condo, he dropped his bags and went straight to the answering machine, hoping that Nancy had called. He was disappointed before it occurred to him that if he didn't know the phone number at the condo, she probably didn't either. There was no way for her to contact him until he got to the office on Monday.

"Ed is playing you." He read the note again after smelling it to see if it held any reminder of her. She had known about the transfer to North Dakota, she had known that Ed had been playing up to him all week. What else did she know? Was she part of the grand scheme? Did Ed ask his niece to snuggle up to the hayseed from Georgia to help convince him to take the transfer? He didn't want to put himself down, but she was honestly way out of his league. Women like that seemed to end up with guys who made a lot more money than he did. Thinking back to the first day at the bar, he realized she became very interested in him very quickly, maybe too quickly. As he sat in the little condo a thousand miles to the north, thinking of his week on Captiva, it all started to smell bad.

***

At a little bistro off the beach, sipping a glass of wine, Nancy told Sam about her week. Sam had always been her one friend who might not agree with her actions, but whom she could count on to be both non-judgmental and brutally honest. Nancy told Sam she was done being Ed's little harlot and was about done with Ed.

She told her about the cute guy from St. Simons and the horrible way she had acted. She talked about the way Jack had looked at her and their first innocent kisses. She told her what a gentleman he had been and about his modest charm. She told Sam how badly she felt about the mess that she had created and how badly Jack would be hurt when he eventually found out the truth.

Samantha leaned back in her chair and stared across the table and the woman she had known for eleven years. "Oh my god, Nancy. You're in love!"

Nancy's face twisted slightly. "Screw you. You know I'm not even capable of falling in love."

Sam laughed. "Time changes shit. You're in love. If I told you that Jack was standing twenty feet behind you right now, would you be sitting at this table or running into his arms?"

Nancy didn't answer.

"Have you listened to yourself?" Sam continued. "When you talk about Ed, all I hear his spite and rage. When you talk about Jack, it's compassion and sympathy. You're in love, and I think you know it."

"I can't love a guy like Jack," said Nancy.

"Why?" asked Sam. "Because he doesn't have millions? Because you might have to get a real job and live in a three-bedroom house in the suburbs?"

Sam leaned forward. There was something she had wanted to say to Nancy for years and there had never been a better time than right at that moment. It might end their friendship, but it needed to be said. "Nancy, you've always thought you were incapable of falling in love because you've always chased guys who were un-loveable. You've always gone for the best looking or richest guy in the room, the guy with the biggest ego, just to feed your own self-image. You can love a man, and he'll love you back. But not the losers you've chased. Just once, go after a man based solely on how he makes you feel, not based on the size of his bank account or the type of car he drives. Find the right guy, not your vision of the perfect guy."

Nancy gave her an ugly look, a mean and spiteful look. Sam braced herself for the coming verbal retaliation but watched as Nancy's face went from anger to a strange, warped, questioning look before she broke down in tears.

***

Jack spent the weekend wrestling with the North Dakota decision. He decided to consult a trusted old friend. He pulled out his guitar and sat out on the condo's tiny deck. He thought about his years on St. Simons and remembered wonderful sunset walks with old summer flings. He missed that old island, and he wished he had never left the ocean. He wanted to find a way to follow his emotions, to go back and live that carefree lifestyle, to live the way he used to. He strummed his guitar, playing with some lyrics, sort of a love song to that old island, but after ten minutes, a neighbor yelled at him.

He could imagine his father's advice about the job, saying, "That's one hell of an opportunity." But his father had only worked for one company from the time he left the Army to the day he retired. Jack walked down to a coffee shop and tried writing a list of the pros and the cons associated with the transfer, but all he did was doodle on his yellow pad as he thought about the thirty-six hours he had spent with Nancy.

Could she really be part of it? How did she know Ed was playing him and what was her role in it? Ed had wasted no expense in persuading him. Was she just another expense? Had he just fallen for a call girl? If she was legit, would she call him like she promised? The questions came faster than the answers.

Before going to bed on Sunday night, Jack laid out the clothes he planned to wear to his first day at the office. He even ironed his shirt, something he only did a few times a year, and usually not for work. A little after 5am, he woke up in a sweat. North Dakota, the thought of the wind-swept plains and the freezing rain, hit him like a fatal disease. He got out of bed and went to the kitchen, where he found the last beer of the original six-pack.

By 6am, the sun was starting to rise, and with the light of day, several things seemed to become clearer. Jack realized that he hadn't spent the weekend weighing the pros and cons of the transfer; he had spent the entire weekend trying to talk himself into it. As he stood out on the deck in the cold morning air, it was clear that he wasn't going to North Dakota. He also realized that making that decision was probably the end of his career with Baxter-Hutton. The only thing left to decide was now what?

When the phone rang at 7:15, he was certain it was Ed calling to get his decision. Before he picked up the phone, he promised himself to be straightforward, honest, and unswayable. There was nothing Ed could say to change his mind. He picked up the receiver and with great confidence said, "Good morning."

There was a long pause before he heard a soft voice with a southern accent say, "Hi, Jack."

***

Ed had breakfast with Brad Reynolds, the manager of his Pittsburgh office and a few of his key employees. He was bragging about how he had convinced Jack to take over the problems in North Dakota with a little wine and some stroking of his ego. "Did he accept the position?" asked Brad.

Ed brushed some crumbs off his suit pants. "He will today. He was just making me wait the weekend so he could ask for more money. He's not going to get it, but I applaud him for playing the game."

Brad shook his head. "I don't know, Ed. The guy seemed to take it as quite a shock. He left the bar the other morning looking like a whipped puppy."

"I'll bet you five hundred dollars that he calls me before ten this morning to take the job," said Ed with a taunting look.

Brad had two daughters in college and couldn't really afford to lose five hundred dollars, but he knew that not taking the bet would result in a good deal of ridicule from Ed. "I'll take that, and when he doesn't call you by ten, we can go double or nothing that he either doesn't call by the end of the day or he turns you down."

Ed gave a big laugh that caused the other customers in the restaurant to turn. "I like it," he said in a booming voice. "Way to step it up, Reynolds!"

***

Hearing Nancy's voice, Jack's mouth went dry. He didn't know what to say. He wasn't prepared for her call, so he remained silent. "Jack, I've done some terrible things, but I can't begin to tell you how much you've come to mean to me in a very short period of time. I don't want you to hate me. In fact, I think I want just the opposite." She paused, but there was no reply. "I don't want to talk about all this over the phone. I want to talk to you in person. I'm going to fly to Wilmington. Will you see me tonight? Can we just talk?"

"I won't be here," was his only reply.

"You took the job in North Dakota?" she asked in a surprised tone.

"No, I didn't, and that probably means that I need to find a new job. I'm going to load up my Jeep and head south. I need to think."

"How far south?" she asked.

"I don't know," he said quietly. "Georgia, Florida, maybe the Keys."

"Jack, I'm in Miami," she said excitedly. "Please come see me. I'll wait for you. Write down this number."

CHAPTER SEVEN

Southward

Jack showered and dressed in a pair of shorts, his flip-flops, and a tropical shirt. He loaded the few possessions he had brought north with him into his Jeep, unbolted the top, and found a guy in the parking lot to help him take it off and stash it in the garage.

He didn't know if he was going to go as far south as Miami, and if he did, he wasn't sure if he would make the effort to call her. "She has done some awful things." Jack suspected there was far more to Nancy then he had suspected. As he drove, he thought of her, her smile, her laugh, her kisses. She was going to be a hard one to get off his mind.

As he headed south on I-95, it was chilly through Virginia. On a whim, he hit the Outer Banks, a trip he hadn't made in years. The diversion would add a day or more to his trip, but he wasn't in a hurry to get anywhere. The mist hanging over Currituck Sound lifted as he crossed the Wright Memorial Bridge from Point Harbor to Kitty Hawk.

His drive down the banks was predictably slow, but the Atlantic Ocean to his left was peaceful and calming. Driving down that coast road heading south, he felt almost drunk with the smell and the feel of the sea breeze. At Hatteras, he lucked out, getting right on the ferry. He made Ocracoke by sunset and then drank the night away at sMacNally's Bar & Grill. At the bartender's suggestion, he stumbled a couple of blocks to the

Crews Inn Bed & Breakfast, where he fell asleep to the grumbles of a squall.

Waking up without a hangover, Jack enjoyed a great breakfast served by a very talkative but pleasant woman. He tossed his bag over his shoulder and walked back down to the bar to find his Jeep where he left it, covered in dew but otherwise untouched. He took the Cedar Island ferry on a morning that was bright and clear. The ride across the sound was refreshing and beautiful. All those things behind him—North Dakota, Ed, Baxter-Hutton—never crossed his mind. The woman ahead of him did.

The temperature had warmed from "a little cool" to "incredibly pleasant." The Carolina coastline was all flowers in the spring, and the dogwoods and azaleas seemed to be on parade. Live oaks hugged the highway through the cool blackwater swamps as he rode through a seemingly endless canopy of shade.

On Pawley's Island, just a few miles from Georgetown, a squall came blowing up Winyah Bay. Jack was fortunate enough to find an old barn that gave him shelter from the fierce low-country storm. It quickly passed and an hour later he had Charleston in his rear-view and Savannah in his sights. He was going to party down on River Street that night!

He called a college buddy, Mike, and invited him and his wife, Peggy, to join him for dinner. He bought them a nice meal at Fiddler's Crab House and they listened to him recount his rather bizarre last two weeks. After dinner, they wandered down River Street, hitting some of his favorite old haunts.

Mike made a point to mention that it was a week night, so just one more and they had to "git." He used the same lie before ordering every beer all night long. Peggy was a good sport and followed the two from bar to bar, making sure they had a good time while reminding them to pay the tab before they left, and picking up Jack's wallet after he left it on the bar.

He slept in the spare bedroom of their apartment, and when he got up, he found a note next to the coffee pot saying he was welcome to stay as long as he needed. He jotted a note back to them saying, "Thanks for everything. There's nothing more important than friends. See you again soon, Jack."

Back on I-95, he made good time until he had his fill of the wind and the traffic. He took the South Newport exit onto Highway 17 to slow things down. Glancing at the sun, he knew he would be on St. Simons about lunch time.

Turning onto the Golden Isles of Georgia felt like he was returning home. Nostalgia greeted him with every passing scene. Here he felt protected from the cold and harsh winters he had imagined in Delaware and North Dakota. The islands were familiar, a sanctuary in his mind. It was as if nothing bad could happen here.

Walking into the Crab Trap on St. Simons, it felt like he had been gone for years, even though it had only been a week and a half. He was thrilled to see John was pouring drinks, Pat and Tara were sitting at a table near the back, Bobby and Pat and Clive were hunkered up to the bar. Across the room sat Annie and Doris. Boy, could that woman fill a t-shirt. She had a pair a full house couldn't beat, he thought to himself.

He visited with all of them. When they asked about his return, he simply said he was rethinking his move and wasn't sure what his future held. It was the truth.

St. Simons held so many pleasant memories, they meandered through his mind like the tidal creeks winding through the marshes. He could have stayed in St. Simons, but something drew him south. He wasn't sure if it was the woman in Miami or the call of the Keys, but his instincts told him to keep moving that direction.

With no real options, he jumped back on I-95 for a few miles down to the Laurel Island Parkway, which he knew would lead him around the southern end of the Kings Bay Naval Base, through the town of St. Marys, and down to the Cumberland Sound ferry.

The ride reminded him of his love for boats and his love for the waters around the Florida-Georgia line. Turning south into the mouth of the Amelia River, the ferry's captain tooted a salute to an inbound submarine. Standing at the rail, Jack was amazed by the size of the sub and commented about it to a couple standing next to him.

"She's a boomer, Ohio-class," said the man. "I served aboard the Tennessee years ago." Jack turned and shook his hand, thanking him for his service.

From the southern ferry terminal, it was on to Fernandina for a round of pirate's punch with some vacationing tourists at The Palace, a fine little saloon he loved, just a block up from the water. Enjoying the sunny day, he picked up A1A and drove down Amelia Island, crossed onto Little Talbot Island, and made the Mayport ferry to cross the St. Johns River. Passing the beaches at Neptune, Jacksonville, and Ponte Vedra wasn't easy, but he had never been down the Guana River stretch of the highway, so he was excited to see it.

It was amazing, the river on his right, the Atlantic on his left, miles and miles of empty, untouched beaches that had been saved from condo developers, like Ed and his buddies, by a stroke of a pen. The twelve thousand acres of uplands had been purchased by the state of Florida in the mid-eighties and forever designated an aquatic preserve.

The Usina Bridge and Vilano Causeway brought him back to the mainland, and back to civilization, but he knew just what to do. A mile south of the causeway, he made a left-hand turn and crossed the Bridge of Lions. Minutes later, he saw the Conch House Lounge and could think of no better place to spend what was left of a wonderful afternoon.

Over the years, the Conch House had become one of his favorite bars. Overlooking the Salt Run Inlet just south of St. Augustine, it had always reminded Jack of those funky little places down in the Caribbean. Roofed by palm fronds and cypress logs, the place tipped its hat to both the local customs and those of the Everglades.

Every time he walked into the Conch House, Jack was reminded of two people. Dean, a buddy from college, and Erin, a girl from Boston that he had met there one afternoon a few years ago. He knew neither of them would actually be there, but he couldn't stop himself from hoping.

During their junior year at Georgia Tech, Jack and Dean had cooked up a big road trip, a final hurrah before they started a busy senior year and then entered the "real world." They were going to go see the country, to make the highway their home. Neither of their parents thought it was a prudent idea, but six weeks before school started in the fall, Jack quit his summer job as a fishing guide. They loaded Jack's '69 MG with a couple of sleeping bags and a cooler of beer and took off without a plan or a destination. Driving south, one of their first stops was at the Conch House Lounge.

Their six-week drive took them across the southern U.S. to see a world that neither had seen. They drove west to California and then south along the Pacific into Mexico. They didn't have a dime to spare between them, but they felt so free heading down the road. Together they witnessed the beauty of a cool Pacific morning and the magic of friendly strangers' smiles. They were living wild and loose and crazy, checking out the scenery and racking up the miles. On the way back east, near New Orleans, Dean said goodbye. The rich girl in La Jolla was calling him back there. Jack went back to college. Dean never did.

There would never be such a short period of time that influenced Jack's life like those six weeks. He learned to slow down, take the road by the water, and to notice and appreciate the incredible tapestry that passed by his driver's side window on every future road trip.

A few years later, as Jack drove home from Dean's funeral in Miami, he reminisced about Dean and their summer road trip. Jack was driving the road by the water, stopping into all his favorite haunts, and in St. Augustine, he stopped at the Conch House. He quietly toasted Dean by slightly raising his beer to the window overlooking the water, and there, across the bar, a beautiful woman was smiling back at him. He told the bartender, "Hey, get that woman whatever she wants."

She had come over to introduce herself and thank him for the drink. He in turn introduced her to their honeydew daiquiris. The happy-hour crowd had started to thin when a group of shrimpers arrived, one of yelling, "Let's get this party underway!"

When he told Erin that he had to get going, that he was due on St. Simons that night, she convinced him to stay. They drank gallons of honeydew daiquiris; Erin's girlfriends took over the bar. The shrimpers yelled out, "Play more Buffett" to a guy named Sunny Jim who was playing guitar.

For a Thursday night, things kept winding up. A group of rowdy divers on their way to Key Largo stopped in in search of women and beer. Some guy kept buying rounds of tequila, and there were bodies all over the pier.

The party finally broke up around midnight. Jack and Erin looked, but her girlfriends were gone. They went for a drive down the coastline and found an empty beach, where Jack spread a blanket. Erin looked out to the surf and suddenly said, "Let's go swimming." They skinny-dipped in the moonlight and woke up wrapped in the blanket in the dunes at dawn.

Jack had always been amazed at how close they had felt for such a brief encounter, but neither of them had thought to ask why. She told him to call her if he was ever in Boston, then kissed him and told him good-bye. He had watched her walk away in the sunrise, then he headed back up the coast. He had reached into the cooler in the backseat, took out an early morning beer, and made her a toast.

***

He took the same seat at the bar he had sat at that Thursday afternoon, so many years ago, hoping against hope that Erin would be sitting with her friends near the window, or that somehow Dean would be there to buy him a beer and tell stories late into the night.

Jack struck up a conversation with a couple next to him, Brian and Gretchen. He told them he was on his way south but didn't know where he was going and didn't really care. They were fascinated by the idea of driving without a destination or a timeline. They invited him to join them for dinner, and without intending to, he spilled his guts about the job in North Dakota, about Ed, and about Nancy.

Talking through his problems, out loud for the first time, seemed like throwing gas on the fire. He could either drown his emotions in alcohol or get away somewhere that he could think, which seemed like the healthier choice. He thanked Brian and Gretchen for their hospitality, took one last look around the bar for the ghosts from his past, paid for the couple's dinner, and left.

He drove down to Anastasia Beach, took his old guitar out of its case, and started walking in the dark looking for a quiet place to sit and play and think. Not far from the parking lot, a group of people gathered around a beach fire laughing and drinking. He walked past them on the oceanside of the beach, giving the group ample berth but still visible to them in the firelight.

"Hey, guitar guy," yelled a man from the group, "come play us some songs."

Jack waved back and said, "I don't do that."

Two ladies who looked like they were in their mid-twenties got up and ran over to him. "Come join us. Play a song or two, and we'll trade for a couple of glasses of sangria." He tried to say no, but they were incredibly persistent, and both very pretty. He finally agreed to try a song but made it clear that the only thing worse than his guitar playing was his horrible voice.

Sitting on a log, he nervously strummed at his guitar. It seemed that every song he had ever learned, even those he had known since he was a kid, had just vanished from his head.

"Let's see, you got your C string, and you got your D string, and you got your G strings," he said to the people staring at him from around the fire while searching his memory for a song to play. "Everybody check your G-strings." The laughter eased his nerves and two decades of music came pouring back into his head.

He started by playing James Taylor's "Sweet Baby James." At the first chorus, the entire group joined in. They urged him to play another, so he said, "Here's a song about sex on the floor," and played "Navaho Rug" with a little more confidence. Everybody applauded. Somebody handed him a glass of sangria and he hoisted it up, saying, "Here's to my first paid gig." The entire group erupted in laughter.

He played them "Mr. Bojangles," "Hill Country Rain," "Contrary to Ordinary," "Into the Mystic," and "Pancho and Lefty" before he ran out of songs he knew by heart. When he admitted that was all he knew, they asked him to play them again and the second time through his "set," they sang even louder. Jack had a blast.

People started wandering away from the fire not long after the sangria, beer, and wine ran out. Jack said goodnight and strolled back up to his Jeep, then drove to his motel just south of town. He had a smile that wouldn't go away.

Waking early the next morning, Jack pointed south and drove for an hour before stopping at a Waffle House for breakfast. It was six or seven hours to Miami, and if he pushed, he could be there by early afternoon, but he wasn't sure he was in any sort of hurry.

He took A1A down to Port Orange before kicking over to Highway 1. Stopping at a grocery store in Oak Hill, he ate his lunch at an overlook just off Mosquito Lagoon. He joined back up with A1A near Cocoa Beach but abandoned it near Fort Pierce.

Near Palm City, he stopped for gas and decided he couldn't put it off any longer. He reached into his pocket for the crumpled piece of paper and dialed the number on it. She answered after the second ring. He told her he was about an hour north of Miami but didn't say much more. She quickly gave him directions to the St. Regis Bal Harbour Resort on North Beach. He agreed, at the very least, to meet with her.

Pulling into the hotel turned his stomach. The place smelled of Ed's money. His Jeep was completely out of place and he was dressed in wrinkled shorts and a casual button-down beach shirt. "Park it somewhere close," he told the smartly uniformed valet. "I don't think I'll be here very long."

She was sitting at the bar dressed in a tight white dress that accentuated her tan. Her hair was up, showing off her shoulders and neck. He had tried to paint an ugly picture of her in his mind, but all his brain said was, "Damn, she looks good!"

"Jack!" she said as she came off her barstool and ran to him. She hugged him tight, and he sort of put his arms around her. "Come sit down," she said. "What are you drinking?"

He asked for a water and when the bartender inquired what kind of water, he said, "Forget it, I'm good" with a bit of a bark.

Nancy looked at him. She could tell he was angry and that he didn't want to be there. She knew she had just minutes before he left. "Jack, I'm not even going to pretend. I'm going to tell you the truth and if the truth isn't good enough, then I'm going to live the rest of my life with regrets. Ed asked me to get close to you on Captiva. He wanted you to feel good about yourself, your job, me, everything. He thought if everything was going really well in your life, you'd take the transfer to North Dakota. But somewhere in those two or three days, I found I really liked you."

Staring out at the ocean, Jack asked quietly, "You're not his niece, are you?"

"No."

"So, you're a hooker, a call girl? Somebody who gets paid to make fools out of guys like me?"

Nancy reached over to take his hand, but he pulled it back. “No, Jack. I’m not a hooker, and Ed didn’t pay me to snuggle up to you. I’m something far worse. Until a week ago, I was Ed’s girlfriend.”

***

In her first week and a half on Key West, Mary Jane had found a room to rent in the back of a bed and breakfast off Whitehead Street. If she helped with breakfast and cleaning rooms, her rent was cut in half by the nice couple, John and Kathy, who owned the place. She took a four-night-a-week waitressing job at the Six-Toed Cat, and with a little more flirting with the manager of the Schooner Wharf Bar, she felt like she might land a bartending job there. She quickly learned that a car, with parking at a premium, was a pain in the ass, so she sold it to a lady stationed at Naval Air Station-Key West and bought a bicycle.

Even better, she had been on three dates with Greg, a catamaran captain on one of the island’s many booze cruise boats. Greg seemed genuine, a nice guy with a mysterious past, but he had a steady job, all of his teeth, and he didn’t ask her to pay half their dinner bill. He thought “Mary Jane” sounded like a Kansas farm girl and decided to shorten her name to Janie. The name stuck, and before long, everybody knew her simply as Janie. She was fine with that: new life, new name.

***

Jack stood up without a word and started walking towards the door. “You didn’t feel something too?” she asked. “You didn’t think there was an immediate, incredibly intimate, and unexplainable bond between us? Jack kept moving towards the door. “You think that day at Cayo Costa was just an act?”

Jack walked out the door but stopped in the hallway. He didn’t know what to believe, but walking out was a final act. He’d never come back and what if he was wrong? He turned around and she was standing in the doorway, a tear coming down her cheek.

"Jack, I'm an ass. I can't ever ask you to trust me, I've ruined that and taken that off the table. But maybe you can learn to judge me by my actions. I'm here with you, not in Wilmington with Ed. That's got to count for something."

CHAPTER EIGHT

I Hear Key West Calling

The Gold Coast zoomed right past him. It was all downhill from there. Jack kicked back as he cruised down A1A. Key West was calling him in a voice that was so loud and clear, it was the last resort and he was heading all the way. He could envision those smiling islands shining in the sun, Matecumbe, Big Pine, and Ramrod Key. At Florida City, he took a left onto Card Sound Road to avoid the traffic down US-1 this time of day. When he saw the waters of the Florida Keys, he realized that if he had come this far, he wasn't going back.

It occurred to him that he had never called Ed with a response to his generous job offer, and despite it all, that was just wrong. With a cold beer in his hand, he made a call to Pennsylvania from Alabama Jacks.

When Ed got on the phone, Jack said, "Hi, Ed. Hey, I'm down here in the Keys and I think I've decided to stay. That job you gave me, I'm giving it back."

"You're making a hell of a mistake, Jack," said Ed in his big booming voice. "You won't get another job in this industry as long as I have any say."

Jack smiled. "Oh hell, Ed, I know I'm making a mistake. I honestly appreciate the opportunity you gave me, but it just doesn't fit my life right now. And it's just a job. I'll get another one someday, better than that one. I got a little off course, but I feel like my life is right back on track."

"I don't think you understand the gravity of this decision," said Ed in an attempt to sway the conversation back his way.

"Actually, Ed, it was an easy choice. I got one of those things that money can't buy. I've got my freedom and I've got my sanity. Oh, and by the way, your girlfriend says hello."

Nancy smiled at Jack. She really was a beautiful woman, he thought.

"My girlfriend? Is that where Nancy's been?"

"Yeah, we're having a great time down here, but don't take it too hard. You'll get another one, not as good as this one. Life seems to ebb and flow, Ed."

"You tell that gold-digging bitch that..."

Jack cut him off. "Good to chat with you too, Ed, and if I didn't mention it before, my girlfriend says hello." Jack hung up as the voice on the other end of the line seemed to explode. He turned to Nancy and said, "Let's go to Key West."

They drove the length of the Keys without hardly talking. At the first bank she could find, Nancy used her American Express card and took the largest cash advance she could, knowing that Ed would shut her card down at any time. She considered it a severance package for both herself and Jack.

Within a few days, they found a tiny apartment to rent. Nancy took a front desk night job at a small hotel and Jack got a job making margaritas in a little bar by the pier. Slowly, the flame that had been extinguished started to smolder again. They started to laugh again, they started to romance each other again, and slowly, they started to trust again.

Despite a very tight budget on their tiny incomes, life was easy. Nancy was falling for Jack in a big way and was enjoying the time they had together. When their schedules aligned, they enjoyed time the beach or shared a cheap bottle of wine on the rooftop deck of the apartment building as Jack serenaded her with his guitar. She was careful to never mention Ed or her life in Wilmington and Jack seemed to be more secure in their relationship each day.

As good as things were, in the back of her mind, she still looked towards her future. She felt like they were just drifting at that moment in time. Not getting ahead, not securing their future, just surviving each day. She also feared losing Jack. She had never been in love and while she tried her best to call it something else, and while she had never spoken the word to him or anybody else, she knew she was falling hard for him. She knew that losing him would be devastating, and that frightened the hell out of her. She was the queen of failed relationships, but none of them had ever been emotionally difficult. One would end, another would start.

Jack was living the dream. His only responsibilities were to show up to work on time and keep his customers happy. They threw twenty-dollar bills his way as he pushed drinks across the bar. He didn't worry about structural design, physics, metal fatigue, or linear friction. When he wasn't working, he spent his time fishing, lying in the sun, or playing his guitar.

His life was complete; he had a dream life and a beautiful girlfriend. He worried about Nancy, however. She had become used to more, and at times, she seemed to look dreamily at a passing yacht or commented about how she missed nice dinners out while they shared barbecued chicken and rice in their little apartment. He was afraid that if he couldn't eventually give her some of the nicer things in life, she might move on, and he was really starting to like her a lot.

Nancy had seemingly dropped Ed from her memory, or at least she never mentioned him. She looked at Jack like he was her everything. Even when she came home from her night shift at the hotel, she was happy to see him. They walked around town hand in hand, she helped him with lyrics to songs that he wrote, and endlessly listened to him play his guitar.

Nearing the end of his shift, the bar became unusually crowded, creating a big job for one bartender. Jack decided to stay an extra hour or so to help out the bartender, a good guy he knew only as Busch. The tips were good, so he didn't mind. As the crowd started to clear out, Jack was clearing tables when two men came in and sat near the rail. It was clear to him that they weren't tourists. One was white, the other Hispanic. The two weren't large or imposing figures and they didn't act threatening in any obvious way, but Jack knew they were dangerous men.

"Hi, what can I get you?" he said as he approached the table.

"Jack?" asked the surprised white guy.

The man looked vaguely familiar. At first, Jack couldn't put a name to the thin and scarred face. Then his eyes opened wide and he said, "Charlie! My God, how the hell are you?"

Charlie reached out and shook Jack's hand, and in a quiet voice, he said, "I got to tell you, man, they call me John down here." He motioned to the man across the table. "This is my friend, Angel."

Jack nodded to him, noticing that he didn't hold out his hand for a shake. "Charlie, or John, and I go back to elementary school. I haven't seen you in years. How the hell have you been?"

"I'd love to catch up with you, man. Angel and I have a little business to discuss, but if you can stick around a bit, I'll let you buy me a beer."

Loitering around the bar, Jack couldn't help but notice the conversation between Angel and Charlie was heated but not loud. When Angel got up to leave, he walked towards the door, then turned around and pointed his finger at Charlie as if to emphasize some point, then he turned and left.

Jack opened two beers and set one in front of Charlie before sitting down across the table. "Everything okay?" Jack asked.

"It's fine," said Charlie. "Some people just have a hard time remembering what they said a week ago. What the heck are you doing down here?"

Summarizing the years since they last saw each other was easy. Jack went to college, got a job, lived on St. Simons, then quit a month ago and moved to the Keys. Charlie's summation was even shorter; he got out of the Army and moved around until he found a way to make some real money.

Jack was intrigued. "How do you make real money down here?"

Charlie glanced around, then leaned forward a bit. "I supply weed to the entire south end of the Keys."

"Damn, Charlie. Are you serious?"

He smiled. "Yeah. It's a good gig if you don't mind dealing with some real a-holes."

Jokingly, Jack asked, "Do you need a good assistant?"

Charlie's smile went away. "If you're serious and willing to take some risks, I know they are looking for a good boat guy to help move product from somewhere out there to here. You know boats, you could easily do it."

"I don't know if I'm all that serious," said Jack. "But just out of curiosity, what do you suppose it pays?"

Charlie shrugged. "I don't know, but it's got to be four or five thousand a trip, maybe more."

***

With Charlie's recommendation, and an incredibly thin pool of willing and available captains, Jack was quickly brought on to make runs to meet a boat or a plane somewhere in a remote area of Keys.

He met a crusty old guy named Ken Hopkins at the Circle K. Together they drove onto Big Coppitt Key and down a long row of older houses to a home that looked vacant, the weeds taking over the minimal landscaping of the 1960's era home. A sun-faded sign lying in the front yard said "H&H Charters, Home of the Big Ones." The home's paint and the roof both needed attention.

Jack followed Ken around to the back of the home where a broken down 32-foot Springer sport fishing boat named *Lucky Strike III* lay tied to a questionable pier.

The "*Strike*" had once been a beautiful boat. Jack had seen a few around the islands that had been well taken care of, but this one had been neglected for years. Her once shiny fiberglass hull was dull and stained. Her stainless-steel riggings had given way to rust many years ago. The wood decking was gray and rotted.

Captain Ken pulled open the engine hatch and checked the oil while Jack poked his head in the cabin. The cabin stank of leaking sewage, rotting garbage, and oil and exhaust. Up in the cockpit, Jack was surprised that the vinyl upholstery had been allowed to rot away in the salt air and sun. Several of the gauges were missing.

"The owner lost the key," Ken said with a wink as he twisted two wires together. "Connect these two, that's your ignition, and then I jerry-rigged a starter switch that just hangs down here." He pushed the plunger button and the motor started turning over. A few seconds later, it caught and started billowing a cloud of black smoke that drifted across the canal, momentarily obscuring the houses on the other side. They cast off and slowly idled out of the marina.

Once clear, Ken turned the wheel over to Jack and lit a cigar. "You seem like a bright guy," said Ken between puffs. "Are you bright enough to stay out of jail?"

Jack smiled. "I don't know. Do you have any tips?"

Ken laughed. "You're bright and you're willing to listen. Where did they drag you up?"

"I'm just a broken down but respectable bartender," quipped Jack.

"Yeah, I got some tips," said Ken. "First of all, figure out how much money you need to make. Divide that by the number of trips you have to make. When you've made that many trips, cash out and get out. Two more trips to get you set up and I'm done. I'll have enough money to pay off my ex-wife and the IRS, then I'm out of here, assuming we don't get caught."

Jack looked back at the weathered old man. "How many trips have you taken?"

"Twenty-six," said Ken.

"And you've managed to stay out of jail. What's the trick?"

"Well, I'm going to show you. The first thing you need to do is spend a lot of time out here fishing so the boys in blue get used to seeing you. The next thing we're going to do is go out and act really suspicious to see if the Coasties will board us."

Jack thought he was joking. "Intentionally?"

"Damn right," said Ken through a hoarse cough. "This is only the second time we've used this boat. We're just a couple of guys out fishing. If they board us, they will leave you alone for a month."

They drifted off Round Key for about forty minutes until a Coast Guard helicopter flew near them, then Captain Ken hit the throttles and made a run towards Old Finds Bight, looking over his shoulder often at the approaching chopper while changing direction from time to time. When the Coast Guard overflew them, Ken made a 90-degree right turn towards Saddlebunch Channel. "If that doesn't do it, nothing will." He shut off the motor and they drifted for nearly an hour, fishing and waiting for a patrol boat to appear.

"Now that right there is the problem with the United States Coast Guard," said Ken in an agitated voice. "You just can't count on them. They'll show up at the most inopportune time, but if you're sinking or trying to look suspicious, they just flat ignore you." He checked his watch. "It's time to go meet the plane."

Their northerly course took them towards a low-lying string of islands, which Ken pointed out as the Outer Narrows above Snipe Keys. Along the way, he also pointed out landmarks and areas to avoid because of shallow waters or coral heads. They rounded the north end of Big Snipe and motored slowly through the narrows. Once clearing the narrows, Ken spun the boat back around a hundred and eighty degrees and re-entered the strait. About halfway through, he cut the engine and told Jack to go drop the anchor, rig a fishing rod, and grab a couple of beers from the cooler. They were just two guys out fishing.

Lightning cracked in the western sky. A squall was fast approaching but looked like it would pass just to the north of them. There was a noise above the rumble, and moments later, a seaplane passed overhead. Ken took off his hat and told Jack to do the same; it was the all clear signal, he explained. The plane banked around and landed in the narrows, then taxied towards them. At Ken's command, Jack tossed three bumpers off the stern as Ken slowly backed the boat towards the plane. A door on the starboard side of the plane opened. Crouching in the door was a pilot, a man as crusty as Ken. He gave a quick wave, then reappeared and started tossing gunny sacks to Jack while Ken held the boat in place. After tossing ten large bags, the unidentified man gave a half wave-half salute, and closed the door. Jack watched as the plane taxied back towards the middle of the narrows.

After the plane took off and disappeared to the south, Jack asked, "Do you ever do this at night?"

"Oh, hell no, that would be dangerous," said Ken. "There's drug runners and sharks and shit out here at night. Remember, we're just a couple of guys out fishing."

They fueled the boat at Sigsbee Marina on Dredgers Key, then dropped the goods in a rowboat hidden in a little mangrove island just off the Florida Keys Community College. After returning the boat to its broken-down berth on Big Coppitt Key, Jack gave Ken a ride back to the Circle K. When he got out of the Jeep, he turned and said, "Not a bad job for a rookie. See you Tuesday." Jack wondered what a "bad job" would have required.

"You're home late," said Nancy as he walked through the door.

"Sorry, I was helping a guy with his boat," said Jack. "How about I shower and we go have a nice dinner out, someplace fancy?" Nancy gave him a questioning look. "This guy who comes into the bar had a problem with his boat he couldn't solve," said Jack. "I fixed it and he gave me a couple hundred bucks. He said it would have cost him a couple of thousand to have it fixed over at the marina."

Nancy smiled. "Fun! I'll get dressed!"

***

The second trip with Ken went as smooth as the first. Ken gave Jack tips on how to deal with the unusual amounts of cash he was about to come into. The drug business was a cash only profession, which was problematic, according to Ken.

Most drug dealers didn't get caught moving drugs; they got caught moving cash, which then led back to the drugs. Banks kept an eye out for large deposits, or series of smaller cash deposits as part of their anti-money laundering requirements. It was best to stash the cash, continue to live frugally, and keep an honest job.

When Jack dropped Ken at the Circle K after their second run, he said, "See you around," to which Ken responded, "No you won't." Jack never saw him again.

Jack decided to keep his job at the bar; his boss and co-workers were flexible enough to allow him certain days off, when he needed to "work his other job." He found an access to the apartment building's attic in the closet of their bedroom and bought an old suitcase at the thrift store for five dollars to stash the cash. He told Nancy he was picking up odd jobs at the marina as a mechanic or fishing guide. She didn't question him. He came home dirty and sweaty, often grease-covered from having to work on the *Lucky Strike III* just to keep her running.

After a few weeks of enjoying his increased income, they decided to upgrade from the tiny apartment to a little house just off Seminary Street. Jack felt like the suitcases of money in the attic of the house would be more secure than the shared attic of the apartment building.

Taking Ken's advice, he continued to work at the bar and they lived very low key, with the exception of some nice meals out and some nice clothes he bought for Nancy. He opened accounts at every bank and credit union on the island and deposited a couple of thousand in cash each month. Tip money, he told the tellers. Despite the deposits, the cash in the attic continued to grow. Nancy took a better job as a receptionist at a law firm. Working days left her with nights free, but Jack often worked at the bar, or hung out in a bar, until after she was asleep.

Jack was loving his life. He was enjoying his free time. His dreams were coming true, he was a tropical man with his toes often in the sand, living in a drunken stupor much of the time. His friends and family would occasionally call from up north; they thought he was throwing his life away in the Keys. But Jack couldn't stop laughing. He felt like he had the whole damn thing figured out.

All was good in Jack's life until his eleventh trip. Returning from a run to Barracuda Keys, the *Lucky Strike III* broke down off Snipe Point. With three hundred pounds of Cuban Electric Lettuce lying uncovered on the cabin deck below, a Coast Guard Patrol Boat came to his "rescue." The Coasties showed up suddenly while he was below in the engine hatch, up to his elbows in a faulty fuel pump. They were beside him and aboard hardly before he knew it.

Luckily, Jack had fishing gear spread around as Ken had suggested, and he was nearly finished with the repair. The Coast Guard Engineer double checked his connections and watched for leaks as he fired her up. As quickly as they had appeared, they were gone. Jack couldn't remember a time when he lived so long without his heart beating.

Arriving at the drop point an hour later, as he went below to retrieve a second bag of pot, two men came out of nowhere, one with a pistol and one with a rusty sawed-off shotgun. Jack quickly assessed the situation. Both men were young and very nervous. In Jack's estimation, the man with the pistol wasn't going to shoot unless his life was threatened. But he was afraid that if the man with the rusty old shotgun pulled the trigger, they would all be killed when the barrel exploded.

Jack could have tried to fight them, but he decided the better course of action was to help them load the dope into their boat. When it was loaded, they turned towards him, uncertain what to do next. Jack offered them a cold beer. Flustered and surprised by his hospitality, they climbed into their boat and left.

Angel was furious that Jack had lost a load and even angrier when he found out that Jack was running his drugs around without weapons, another helpful suggestion from Ken. "Never carry a gun unless you plan on using it," Ken had said.

Sitting on his front porch that night while Nancy worked her last graveyard shift at the hotel, Jack got drunk and decided that making money off the old square grouper wasn't the life for him. The next day, after his hangover, he got a job with one of the local companies as a charter fishing captain. Lacking any original ideas, he decided to call himself Captain Jack.

***

The call came as quite a surprise. Mary Jane hadn't spoken with Jenny since her wedding reception. It was, of course, according to Jenny, Mary Jane's fault that they hadn't spoken, but Mary Jane dismissed it as another rant. Jenny announced that she and Bill were coming to see her in Key West, and by the way, could they stay in her guest room? Mary Jane laughed. She explained that she lived in the back of a bed and breakfast in a glorified broom closet. She'd be happy to make them a reservation.

Jenny seemed put off that she would actually have to pay to stay in Key West but gave her the dates they would be there and then changed her tone and said how excited they were to see her again. Mary Jane hung up. Excited was a good word to explain the coming visit, and interesting would be a good word too.

CHAPTER NINE

Captain Jack

The split Jack worked out with Stock Island Charters was pretty thin because they provided the boat, the fuel, paid the mate, and provided the clients. He made considerably more if he found the clients, and in Key West, that meant spending time where the customers were, in the bars. His marketing plan was simple: hang out in a bar, talk to drunken tourists about the great fishing in the Keys, and sign them up. It turned out to be not that simple.

For several weeks, the winds blew thirty knots from the Northwest. Jack swore that if he was a sailboat captain, there'd be no wind at all. The cold fronts scared the tourists and when he did go out, the fish sure seemed to disappear. It was getting harder to find a client; he'd just as soon find a beer.

Nancy was becoming increasingly frustrated with him as he became increasingly lazy. Jack knew he had to get himself together; he'd been coasting for too long. He would tell those who would listen, "When I get my second wind, stand clear. Captain Jack is coming back, I swear."

He used his "attic money" to purchase a small fishing boat of his own, the *Marauder*, a 28-foot Mako with twin Mercury outboards. She needed a lot of work, but he could do the majority of it himself, and he'd have a great boat and be able to keep a hundred percent of the profits. He told Nancy he had used a small inheritance from his grandfather that he had forgotten about to buy the boat. She didn't seem to care one way or another.

One morning, after drinking too much and sleeping on his boat, he went home to find the little house on Seminary Street empty. Nancy's clothes were gone, and the only trace of her was a note that simply said, "I had to leave, I'll call you soon. Nancy."

At another point in his life, Jack might have handled the news differently, but at that moment, he did the only thing he could think of. He opened a beer. He had more after that one, and before long, he had a midnight buzz at 9 AM.

By eleven, he had made his way down to Turtle Kraals and found a seat at the bar next to a couple vacationing from Detroit. He rambled on to them about fishing, living in Key West, and women that couldn't be trusted. "Those old pros over there laugh about me," he said, pointing to a couple of captains sitting in the corner drinking coffee. "They say I've lost my touch. They say I'd fish a whole lot better if I drank about half as much."

The couple asked for their check. "I'm so damn tired of people, and all the things they say," Jack said as they paid their tab. "I'm going to move closer to bad weather someday and just live alone." The couple got up and left without saying anything. Jack watched them leave, then said to himself, "I've got to get myself together."

***

Bill and Jenny flew from St. Louis to Miami. They rented a car and drove to Key West without stopping once. Mary Jane had to admit, despite it all, she was excited to see them. When they arrived at the bed and breakfast, they all hugged. Jenny even commented on how good Mary Jane looked. She had lost a few pounds, had a healthy tan, and the salt air did something amazing to her hair.

They were excited to see Key West and she was excited to show them. When they came down to the living room, Mary Jane resisted the urge to puke. They had changed into matching golf shirts. She chose not to comment.

Knowing Jenny's need to be the leader, Mary Jane appropriately asked, "Do you want to explore the town on your own and I'll just follow along, or would you like a tour guide today?" Jenny opted for the tour guide, stating that she was ready for the VIP tour. Of course, thought Mary Jane.

They walked over to Duval Street and started up the street, stopping here or there: at a bar for a drink, a gift shop for a trinket, just wandering, visiting, eating and drinking. They were having a nice time.

They made it to Mallory Square about a half hour before sunset, giving them time to see the festivities there: jugglers, mimes, and a comical low wire act. With drinks in hand, they watched an amazing sunset in the western sky. "The world's biggest canvas gets painted every day," said Mary Jane as they watched the blazing orange and yellows of the incredible sunset.

The sunset booze cruise boats started to return. They always made a point to swing in close to Mallory Square so the tourists there could see how much fun everybody on board was having. They each sported their phone numbers painted on the side so the land-lubber tourists could book their own trips.

When a big white catamaran came by, Mary Jane put two fingers to her mouth and made a loud whistle, which bought a toot from the boat's horn and a wave from the white-shirted man at the helm. "That's my boyfriend Greg," she told them. "He'll catch up with us in a bit."

Jenny grabbed her arm. "You have a boyfriend? And he has a big boat?" Mary Jane just smiled and waved for the two to follow her. There were places to go and margaritas to be drunk.

***

After sleeping away most of the afternoon, followed by two cups of coffee and a few aspirin, Jack took a big glass of water and the only friend he had at the moment, his old guitar, and went to the swing on the little porch. It was clearly time to take stock of his life. He wasn't a good drug runner, he wasn't a good fisherman, and he wasn't good at relationships.

He slowly strummed his guitar, remembering the first years he played. He looked at the old guitar; it was the same one his uncle had given him as a kid, a custom built Giltzow. He remembered summer nights, trying to get the chords just right. He worked so hard to play that new guitar.

He would memorize songs and then follow his mom around the house, asking her about his sound. He dreamed of becoming a huge star. Over the years, he grew up and left home, time flew by and life moved on, and he forgot all about his dream. But no matter where he went or what he did, he always dragged around that old guitar.

Sitting on the porch, he played every song he could remember and vowed to learn more. It was time for a change, and while he didn't know what he would change, he knew he had to set a new course in his life, just as soon as he finished playing the next song or two. He played late into the night, and nobody yelled at him.

***

After completing his nightly duties as captain, taking care of his guests, cleaning and securing the boat, and checking on provisions for the following afternoon's run, Greg walked over to Duval Street and started through the usual bars, looking for Janie and her friends. He found them in Sloppy Joes.

When she saw him, Janie ran over, grabbed Greg's hand, and pulled him across the bar to meet her lifelong friends, Bill and Jenny. The bar was loud, it was hard to hear, and everybody was hungry, so they walked a block up Duval and one block over to Two Friends Patio for a bite.

"Janie?" asked Jenny after she heard Greg use the name. "I thought I heard somebody on the street say 'Hi Janie,' earlier. When did you become Janie?"

Greg laughed. “I think that’s my fault. When we met, I told her that Mary Jane sounded like a Kansas farm girl and that I was going to call her Janie. It sort of stuck. So down here, she’s known as Janie.”

Jenny gave the two of them a deeply thoughtful look before saying, “I like it, it suits her!”

After eating, they rolled through the bars along Duval Street, drinking and dancing. It was a beautiful evening; the winds that had plagued the Keys for the last few weeks had died down and the skies had cleared, allowing the full moon to show off its charm.

Jenny asked Greg when they would have a chance to go out on his big boat. Greg explained that it wasn’t his, he was just the captain, but they were welcome to join him anytime as his guests. Jenny jokingly said that she wanted to go sailing now, to see the full moon. Greg cocked his head a little and said, “That’s a pretty good idea. Let’s take my boat out for a moonlight sail.”

Janie jumped up, saying, “Yeah, let’s go!” She was such a good sport because he was such a crazy man.

Greg was twelve years older than Janie and divorced. Most of his income went to pay child support for his two kids up in Pensacola. He lived on a thirty-four-foot Beneteau sailboat, the Papeete, that he could moor for free at a little spot next to the party barge. As much as he loved to sail, he hadn’t untied the Papeete from the dock for more than two months.

He disconnected the shore power, cast off the lines, and expertly backed her out of the slip, and they were underway in minutes. After clearing Key West Bight, Greg turned her into the wind, and with his instructions, Bill, Jenny, and Janie helped raise the sails. He turned her across the wind and cut the engine, and they were sailing, almost silently, across the strait.

Wisteria Island was on their right, Sunset Key would pass on their left. Ahead of them was nothing but dark ocean except for a band of light that ran from their boat, across the ocean, pointing to the horizon below the incredible moon.

They drank wine, they chased moonbeams, and they sang along to favorite old songs coming from the stereo. It was a perfect night. After a few hours, Jenny gave Bill that look, and they went below. In their own throes of romance, Janie and Greg laughed as they felt the boat rocking; they knew why.

Sometime in the early morning hours, the four of them stretched out in the cockpit and enjoyed rum drinks while sitting nearly still in calm winds. A slice of orange started to appear in the eastern sky and they all greeted the dawn with sleepy eyes. The moon and the stars disappeared and spirits aboard the little boat started to sag. But Greg was a professional; he mixed mimosas all around, stating, "You can't drink all day unless you start at sunrise!"

The winds began to blow and soon they were underway, pointed back towards Key West. Janie, wearing one of Greg's t-shirts and a pair of his shorts, walked forward and found her bikini on the deck. She released a halyard and raised the colors on a brand-new day. Her bikini bottoms made such a stylish flag!

***

Waking early, Jack rolled over. Nancy wasn't there. He hadn't expected her to come home, but he could always hope. He got up and pulled on a pair of shorts and a shirt off the floor, then walked out to the kitchen and made a pot of coffee. The day looked nice and the winds seemed to have calmed a bit.

He poured a cup and grabbed his guitar and headed for the chair on the porch. His yellow legal pad had been sitting out there a few days, the edges curled from the humidity. Reading the last lyrics he had written, he thought they sounded like garbage. He started to rip the page from the pad but stopped and re-read them. They weren't bad.

It was something Nancy had said to him in Miami when she was trying to convince him of her feelings for him. "I don't want to go home," she said. "I'll give everything away, I'd rather stay with you instead. I'll make it on my own, I don't need lots of money, I just don't want to go home."

Taking a sip of coffee, Jack penned below the paragraph, "She fell in love with the ocean, it made her feel so free. Sailing every day, sliding over the sea. The sound of the steel pans, and the island melody, left no question in her mind, this is where she needs to be." He read and re-read the words again. It occurred to him that life was a crazy puzzle, and he had stumbled over clues. It was all about his choices, so he'd want to be careful what to choose.

He tried several different ideas but failed to put the words to a melody. He decided to make himself a fried egg sandwich and then go work on his boat. If the winds were starting to die down, there might be some fishing opportunities in the next few days.

***

The three days with Bill and Jenny had been fun and Janie was sad to see them go. She saw both of them in a new light. Jenny wasn't the opinionated, domineering person she had seemingly grown into. She was still the warm and caring friend she had always been, but with high expectations and hopes for those around her. Over their years apart, Jenny had simply found the confidence to voice her expectations. She wanted more for Janie, and she told her so.

Bill had also grown into a nice adult. He was everything Janie had loved originally, kind and polite, respectful, but boring as a rock. Looking at him now, she saw a man who would have been a good and decent husband, a good provider, and a calm and caring father. She now imagined her life with Bill as dull, monotonous, and mundane. She waved as Bill and Jenny left to return to St. Louis and their humdrum life.

Walking along the streets of Key West, she saw the island in a new light. Where before it was a crowded and overpriced tourist trap, she now saw it as a sort of sanctuary, a piece of land protected on all sides by a beautiful ocean. Everywhere she looked was like a picture, miles of beaches, clear water everywhere. She strolled along to the beat of the song that a man sitting on his porch played. Her smile was as big as the sun, and on her face she had what the locals called the Island Daze.

***

Jack didn't notice the woman on the sidewalk, walking, nearly dancing to the beat of the song he was playing. He gave a final strum and set his guitar inside the door. With newfound enthusiasm, he headed down to the yard to work on his boat. The lower ends of both the engines were in pieces, and with some dedication and a little luck, he thought he might be able to get them back together before dark.

Sitting on a bucket in the shade of a palm tree, up to his elbows in grease and a confusing array of parts, Jack hummed songs to himself. He put together lyrics in his head and wished he had a third arm to write them down. He played the melodies and the lyrics over and over in his mind, hoping he wouldn't forget them. Occasionally, he would take a break and jot down a verse or a string of notes while sipping on a beer from the little cooler he brought from the house. Sipping, he reminded himself, not drinking defensively like he had the last few months.

As he worked on the engines, he hummed to himself and thought a lot about Nancy. He wondered where she had gone. Was she back in Wilmington with Ed? Was she back in Miami with her friend, Samantha? Wherever she ended up, he imagined her complaining about the lackluster man she had mistakenly taken up with. The guy who couldn't hardly get out of bed, whose life wasn't going anywhere. He wished she would call or that she would reappear to see how he had changed. He missed her.

The days turned into weeks. Jack continued to work diligently on his boat whenever he had a chance. He picked up a few more fishing charters and even had a little success. He put in a few more hours at Murphy's each week.

One quiet afternoon at the bar, Jack pulled out his guitar and started strumming a tune he had been working on, molding and shaping it. A couple walked in off the street and sat at a table. “What can I get you?” said Jack as he started to get up.

“Nothing at all,” said the lady. “We just stopped in to get out of the sun and hear you play.”

Jack blushed. “I wasn’t really playing. I was just messing around.”

“Well, please keep messing around,” she said with a laugh. “It sounded wonderful. Good enough to get us to stop in.”

Leaning on his guitar for a thoughtful moment, Jack sat back and started strumming the opening chords to Bob Seger’s “Night Moves.” Two women and a man came into the bar during the song and sat close to where he was playing. After finishing the song, he jumped up, took their orders, and refilled some others’ drinks. “Play some more,” yelled a woman.

“I can’t, I’m working,” Jack said with an apologetic smile.

“If you play, I’ll tend the bar,” said the man who came in with the two women. “It’s been a few years, but it’s like riding a bike, right?”

Uncertain how that would go over with the bar’s owner, and wrestling with his own insecurities about playing, Jack resisted. The small group in the bar talked him into one more. He played “Tin Cup Chalice” by Jimmy Buffett, which drew in a few more people. Finishing the song, he glanced over at the bar and saw the man who had offered to tend his bar pouring beers.
He told his tiny audience he would play one more, but then he had to get back to work.

“This is one I’ve been writing. It’s still a little rough but it’s sort of an autobiography of my life so far.” With a smile, he said, “And it goes just-like-this.”

He was three years out of college, a damn good engineer, he worked hard all day, then he partied away, life was happy on the old frontier...."

When he finished the song, the growing crowd erupted in applause. Jack blushed, put down the guitar, kicked the customer out from behind the bar, and refused to play anymore. But as shy and embarrassed as he acted, he felt something welling up inside himself. He had probably never had so much fun as the three minutes singing his own song to a crowd of appreciative people. He knew he wanted to feel that excitement again.

After his shift was over, Jack walked over to the boat yard where he sat on his landlocked vessel and watched the sun go down over the condos and the palm trees to the west. He thought about Nancy, wishing she would call, dreading when she finally would. He reached for his yellow pad and wrote almost a diary entry. "I'm working on my boat, and waiting for your call. I'm living the life of a writer, but most days I don't write at all. I'm fishing for my living, and waiting for the words, but my muse ain't so amusing, it's a voice I've seldom heard."

CHAPTER TEN

Too Early for That Kind of Drinking

People around town had heard rumors about Nancy and seemed to be excited to freely share them with Jack. The most prevalent rumor was that she had taken up with a rich sailor and headed for the islands. She had simply sailed away and was gone for good.

The message on his recorder came a few days later. It simply said, "Hi, Jack, it's Nancy. Give me a call. My number is 555-674-9831." He listened to the message five times, trying to hear some sort of emotion in her voice—a glimmer of sorrow, a shred of affection, even a hint of anger—but he had no idea what her tone indicated. He glanced at the clock. It was just after noon. He decided that it was a little too early for that kind of drinking, so maybe he'd call her tonight.

He decided to walk to Murphy's for a couple of beers, but on his way there, he ran into Giles, a Frenchman who frequented his bar. "Jack, Jack! Come sailing with us," he said in his heavy accent. "The winds are good and we need another body." Giles had been offering to take Jack out on his racing catamaran for months. Sailing seemed a healthier choice than sitting all afternoon with the barflies at Murphy's.

The winds out in the channel were strong ahead of a small front coming from the west. Giles proved his skills as an accomplished captain by flying the hull for long periods of time in the consistent winds, but the ocean's chop made for a rough ride. Jack was essentially just ballast, weight strapped into a harness and hanging off the lee side of the boat to counteract the force of the wind. It looked easy enough; his feet rested on the edge of the deck, his weight was supported by the wire attached to his harness. All he had to do was hang out. But it was anything but easy.

At first, he was convinced the Giles was going to flip the big cat as the hull came out of the water and "flew" four to five feet above the ocean. The boat cut through the swells, slamming the hull down time and time again as they hit the trough. It was a beating. Fun, Jack thought, but not the relaxing booze cruise sailing excursion he had imagined.

As they headed back in, they dropped the sails just outside the bight and Giles brought out rum for everybody. Jack helped Giles hose down and secure the boat after his other guests wandered off.

Giles Boutier was the son of a wealthy French industrialist. When he was in his twenties, he talked his father into letting him take some time away from the family business and go on a little sailing adventure. He never returned home other than to visit. After circumnavigating the globe several times, Giles landed in Key West and had made the little island his home. Now in his late sixties, he told people he planned to die in the Keys. He was a short man with a weathered face and stout chest. His forearms, which were always exposed by his rolled-up sleeves, were both tan and muscular. He loved life, he loved to party, and he loved to sail.

When the winds weren't blowing, he painted: portraits, landscapes, and his favorite, ocean scenes with sailboats. His paintings graced homes up and down the Keys, and they could be found in restaurants and bars. A portrait of Jesus hung in the local Lutheran church. He had never charged a penny for his art.

After securing the aft rigging, Giles sat in the cockpit and motioned for Jack to join him. In his heavy accent, he said, "Jack, how are you doing? I worry about you."

“I’m okay. I got a message from Nancy this morning, and she wants me to call her.”

Giles gave a concerned look. “I saw her in Paris last week. I talked with her and told her that you were well, but sad. I told her that she needed to call you.”

“Paris?” exclaimed Jack. “She’s surely been getting around.” He looked out across the harbor, seeing and noticing nothing. He felt happy for her, that she was doing all the things that she wanted, all the things that she said she would do.

Giles offered to buy him dinner, but he wasn’t in a cordial mood. Jack thanked him for the sail and wandered off, not really going anywhere. He knew he wasn’t acting the way he was supposed to. He was distracted by the “whys” and the “whats,” fighting internal battles and wrestling with his feelings.

Imagining the phone call with Nancy as he aimlessly walked around town, he could hear her voice. She would ask him how he was doing and he would tell her that he had been down, feeling like there was a constant mist on the ocean enshrouding the island. He felt detached and alone.

She would ask if he was still writing, he would say that he was, but the words didn’t come easy and sometimes the effort just wore him out. “I’m a little too pensive, withdrawn and reflective, a little too drab and too gray,” he would tell her. He’d love to see her. He probably needed to, just to set everything straight. He knew he couldn’t change all the things that had happened, and in the end, her leaving was probably nobody’s fault.

Jack’s thoughtless route had taken him in a big circle, bringing him back to the bight, mindlessly drawn to his love of the water and of boats. Walking past Schooner’s Wharf Bar and Turtle Kraals, he heard but ignored the sounds of happy tourists having alcohol-infused fun. For no particular reason, he turned and walked out along the dock where a sunset booze cruise catamaran was returning with a fresh load of drunken revelers.

As the boat eased up to the dock, one of the crew members, a woman holding a line, gave him a head nod and said, "How about a little help?" seconds before she tossed him the bowline. Jack instinctively caught it and walked to the nearest cleat and tossed a perfect cleat hitch around it. "Thanks," said the woman in the white crew shirt. He gave a quick smile back towards the vaguely familiar face. "Jack?" she asked.

He turned and looked back at her. The name came to him immediately, but he couldn't quickly put together the connection of how he knew her or where he knew her from. "Mary Jane?" he asked back.

***

If you could cut through all the armor and peel back the layers, eventually one would find that Nancy was as insecure and uncertain as the rest of the world. It wasn't that she was unable to maintain a loving relationship, or that she had fallen out of love with Jack, but quite the opposite. Even as Jack slid deeper into the island life, despite his drinking and even the drug running, which she knew about, she had loved him without reservation. Which was exactly why she left.

Every relationship Nancy had ever been in had ended badly, so she had no reason to believe this one would be any different. One day, a wealthy man from Spain came into the law firm to sign some documents. Sebastian asked her to join him for dinner on his sailboat, and three martinis later, he asked her to sail away with him to the islands. Two days later, she watched Key West and her relationship with Jack both fade into the horizon.

To Nancy, love was a mysterious, dark, and frightening venture. Taking up with a wealthy man and milking the relationship as long as she could was much more natural and commonplace to her. She knew she was warped beyond help, but Sebastian was a competent lover, he seemed to have plenty of money and was willing to share it, he had a big boat, and made a delicious martini.

***

For a moment, Janie didn't know what to say. She was speechless. The man who had changed her life in a few words, a man she didn't think she would ever see again, was standing on the dock, a few feet from her.

Jack was still trying to put the pieces together. He knew her name and her face, but the encounter was completely out of context.

Janie rushed to the port side stairs, muscled her way past a retiree from Milwaukee, ran up to Jack, and threw her arms around him. "I can't believe you're here! What are you doing in Key West?"

It was starting to come together. St. Louis, this was the woman from that drunken night at the convention. "I've been living down here for a couple of months." He was still blown away by the surprise of seeing her on that boat.

"Don't move," she ordered. "I've got a couple of things to wrap up, but I want to catch up with you." Jack nodded in agreement.

After the guests were gone, the crew started hosing down the boat. Janie told her crewmates she had just run into an old friend. Being the captain's girlfriend, nobody told her she couldn't leave before all the work was done. She walked down the deck towards him with a huge smile. "Come on, I want to buy you a beer!" she said.

Taking him by the hand, she led him a few blocks over to the Smokin' Tuna Saloon where they found a quiet table and ordered two beers. "You know I'm down here because of you," she said as the waitress left their table.

"Was the sex so bad that you were embarrassed to go home?" asked Jack with a bit of a smile.

Janie laughed. "Do you remember what you said to me in the lobby, right before you left?"

Jack tried to remember, but the only thing he really recalled from that morning was the near-death hangover. "I'm sorry, I don't."

"You told me that I had been so focused on red that I had never seen blue. That same night, a sweet old man in a little bar told me that the bluest thing he had ever seen was the ocean down here, so I bought a car and drove down."

"That was an analogy I heard in a church sermon a thousand years ago," Jack said, still not really remembering the conversation. "It wasn't meant to be life-changing advice."

"But you were right," she said with a smile. "I had been so focused on one course that I couldn't see any other. Your advice changed the way I look at life. Hell, it changed my life."
She looked at the sullen and quiet man with the four-day-old beard that sat across from her. He looked sad and tired. "What's your story? Weren't you getting a big promotion and moving somewhere north?"

Leaving out most of the details, he quickly told her about the move to Wilmington, the request to move to North Dakota, and his decision to quit and head for the Keys. Jack looked into her eyes and saw honest concern and understanding, so he told her about Nancy. He told her about the beautiful woman who had left him without warning, and about the message she had left on his answering machine just that morning.

"Are you going to call her back?" she asked.

"I should, just to set everything right," was his only reply.

"Fuck that," Janie replied. "You don't owe that bitch anything. She left you. Why would you give her the satisfaction of making amends for her shitty actions?"

Jack shrugged his shoulders. “Do you really want her back in your life?” asked Janie. “Give a woman like that a week or two and she’ll be out loving someone new. It’s probably happened a hundred times before. Did you really see her as a long-term part of your future?”

Looking across the table at the woman asking the hard questions, Jack noticed such a difference. Nancy was beautiful, elegant, and sexy, but quite frankly, a little shallow and superficial. She was incapable of asking such questions or having more than a one-dimensional conversation. The woman sitting in front of him was very pretty, but in a much more genuine and authentic way. She was beautiful with or without perfect hair and makeup. She was alluring in a much more honest way than Nancy.

He wasn’t prepared to answer her questions, so he changed the subject. “Are you really happy down here? Is your life with the rum boat captain everything you had hoped for? Do you see him as a long-term part of your future?”

Janie smiled at his diversionary tactic. “I am happy down here for now. Greg is fun, for now. This island, this life, and that guy, are all just a stop on my journey. They aren’t my destination.”

“What’s your final stop?” he asked. “Where is Mary Jane headed?”

“That’s the beauty of life,” she said with a wonderful smile. “A nice old man up in Missouri once told me, ‘if you don’t know where you’re going, any road will get you there.’ I’m not sure where I’m going, and as long as I’m happy when I get there, what the hell does it matter?”

She took a drink of her beer and looked at the sullen, broken man across the table. “Several months ago, I was the one who thought my future was dark and bleak. Then this well-mannered southern boy I met in a hotel bar made me see that the world is full of color, full of possibilities. He made me open my eyes for the first time and see the opportunities that could and would present themselves if I would just allow myself to see them. That's why I was so excited, so blown away to see you standing there on the dock tonight. I was afraid I would never have the chance to thank you for the tremendous and surprising changes your twenty-second lesson made in my life."

Jack was shocked. He now sort of remembered telling her the red and blue fable, but he couldn't imagine that anything he ever told anybody would have such an effect on their lives. Her eyes and the tone of her voice held such honesty and sincerity. She made him feel warm and worthy; she made him feel a self-worth that he had lost a long time ago.

"The Keys haven't been good to me," he said to her. "Since I got here, I've done some things that you don't want to know about. I've drank too much, lost a woman I thought I loved, and now I feel like I'm spinning out of control. I need to find a new path, a new direction."

He remembered something she had told him in the St. Louis bar. It would probably be a conversation ender and drive her away, but he didn't guess that this was more than a one-beer discussion to begin with, so what the hell.

"You told me on the evening that we first met, you had found the perfect treatment for the blues."

Janie smiled. "Good tequila and a quick roll in the hay?"

He blushed. "Do you have an interest in helping out a dear old friend?"

Janie spun around in her chair, and he knew he had blown it. He had made the same mistake a hundred times before in a hundred different bars. He had gone too far too quickly.

"Can we get four shots of Patron over here?" she yelled when the bartender looked her way.

***

Jack awoke to the sound of rustling in his bedroom. He opened his eyes and saw her in the pre-dawn darkness pulling on a pair of shorts. "Sneaking out?" he asked with a slight chuckle.

"I've got a really busy day," she said in a soft voice as she moved to his side of the bed and sat next to him. "I need to get over to the B&B to help with breakfast and housekeeping, then I have the lunch shift at the restaurant, and I'm filling in on another sunset cruise this afternoon."

"Wow, that's really ambitious."

She ran her hand softly through his hair. "It's expensive to live in paradise."

He got up on his elbows and looked her in the eyes. "Would you like to go out on a real date with me?"

"Do you mean there is more to you than cheap booze and fun sex?" She laughed. Looking at him for a moment, she said, "Yeah, I think I would like to go out on a real date with you."

"Great, when do you have a free afternoon or evening?"

She leaned over and kissed him. "Wednesday." Then she stood up and walked out of his bedroom.

After she left, Jack did something he hadn't done in a long time; he got out of bed before dawn. He showered, dressed in clean shorts and a button-down tropical shirt, and went for a walk across the island. Something about the day seemed hopeful. As the sun came up, he found himself standing at the water's edge while the daylight sneaked across the sky and the world seemed to come to life before him.

What a perfect morning, what a perfect day, he thought to himself. He felt like he was seeing a new world for the first time as he looked across the water. He was witnessing beauty everywhere he looked. There was some kind of magic on the water and even a whisper of music in the air.

Wednesday couldn't come fast enough. Jack arrived late to pick up "Janie," as everybody knew her in the Keys. The battery on his Jeep had gone dead since he drove it last, a few months earlier. She wore a yellow sundress with a floppy hat that made her look like a sassy southern bell, a look Jack quickly decided he liked very much.

They drove up to Big Pine Key and then turned north before crossing on to No Name Key. Jack knew of a great little beach on the north shore where he had once delivered a load of ganja. Once he found it, he was happy that the beach was empty of both tourists and drug smugglers. He set up a beach umbrella, a little table, and two chairs he had borrowed from his neighbor's backyard. He was sure the elderly couple wouldn't miss their lawn furniture for a few hours.

The wine was excellent, the lunch he had packed—crackers, cheese, and an assortment of fruits—was delicious. They talked for hours, sharing stories and talking about their pasts. When the conversation turned towards their futures, the discussion became awkward and difficult. Janie smiled, then held up her glass in a toast. "Here's to having no future! Live for today because tomorrow may never come!"

After a while, Jack pulled his guitar out of the back of his Jeep. "I didn't know you played," she said in a curiously sexy voice.

"You're about to discover that I don't play, or sing. I apologize in advance." He started to strum the opening chords to one of the songs he knew well but glanced up and saw her eyes. The honesty and sincerity were there again. He abruptly stopped, saying, "You know, life is all about taking chances."

"I agree," she said as he leaned his guitar against the little table, stood up, and raced to his Jeep. She hoped she wasn't being left behind.

Returning with a well-used yellow legal pad, he thumbed back several pages to find what he was looking for, then flipped the pages over to reveal the one he was after. The wind kept blowing the paper around, and after a moment of struggling to keep the pad on the right page, he handed her the pad and asked her to hold it so he could see the words.

"This is a song I wrote after a particularly rough night a month or so ago. I decided it was time to take stock of my life." He strummed a few chords, then paused. "I don't know, maybe it's more than just a song to me. It's an anthem, a psalm that sort of reflects where I've come from and where I think I'm going. I've never played it for anybody." He took a deep breath:

Sometimes on days like this
When the mirror seems so unkind,
I remember the kid playing in the Georgia sun.
His nose in a mystery book,
Playing "pilot" in a magnolia tree,
Shooting down those enemy fighter planes one by one.

Just pretending to be Mickey Mantle,
Hitting rocks in a field by the road,
Or Napoleon Solo living the life of a spy.

I wanted to sail a boat to Tahiti,
Wanted to sing and learn how to fly.
Racing out of control down some open road,
Always dreaming and living till the day I die.

I remember one Easter Sunday,
Waking up in a strange hotel
The whole night's a blank, and I don't know where I am.
In a diner crowded with families

All dressed in their Sunday best,

Some kid points me out and asks "Dad, what's wrong with that man?"

Sometimes life taps you on the shoulder

To remind you it's a one-way street.

You need to do the post mortem on the life that's just passed you by.

I wanted to sail a boat to Tahiti,

Sing and learn how to fly.

Racing out of control down some open road,

Always dreaming and living till the day I die.

Here's hoping that the end comes quickly

When I'm a nimble seventy-five.

Cut down by some young woman's husband who found where I hid.

I don't want to be trapped in a deathbed,

Surrounded by all of my friends,

With time to recall all those things that I never did.

You've got to jump into the arena,

Roll the dice, take some shots to the chin.

You may lose sometime but, hell, you know you've just got to try.

I wanted to sail a boat to Tahiti,

Sing and learn how to fly.

Racing out of control down some open road,

Always dreaming, and living till the day I die.

Yeah, just living till the day I die.

He honestly didn't know what to expect from her when he finished. A rousing applause would have been nice, a look like she had just thrown up in her mouth might have been appropriate, but the blank stare was not what he had hoped to see after he had opened his heart and soul to her with his song.

As the last chord died from the guitar, a single tear formed in the corner of her eye. "What do you call that?" she asked as she wiped away the tear that rolled down her cheek.

"I hadn't really thought about it, but since you seem to like it, how about 'Janie's Song'?"

She smiled. "No, I think you should call it 'Living till the Day I Die.'"

Jack smiled and without a word started playing her another song. As the sun began to set, the mosquitos started to come out, so he suggested they pack up and leave. "Can we just stay for the sunset?" she asked. He hated to refuse her.

They sat quietly for a while, watching the setting sun. After a bit, she glanced over and caught him staring at her with a curious look. "What are you looking at?"

"It just occurred to me, looking at you sitting there. You were raised in the wrong place. It's clear that you're a beach girl at heart, happy when you're near the ocean. You're a child of the summer wind, and you should never be away from the ocean."

Janie smiled and blushed. She wasn't sure if it was a line or if he really meant it, but she liked it.

When the sun was gone, it set the sky ablaze. There was nothing quite as pretty as the twilight time, when the water became inflamed with the image of a sunburned sky.

Standing at the water's edge, Janie looked at the amazing scene before them and said, "The world's biggest canvas…"

Jack smiled, saying, "Gets painted every day."

She gave him a shocked look. "Where did you hear that?" she asked.

Jack shrugged his shoulders. "I don't remember."

***

The economics of the marijuana trade were fairly simple. A guy with twenty pounds would divide it into twenty one-pound portions, and sell it for double what he paid. Whoever bought the one-pound package would divide it into sixteen one-ounce baggies and sell it for double what they paid. The person who bought the one-ounce baggie, if they were going to resell it, would roll it into several joints and sell it for double what they paid.

At these quantities, twenty pounds or less, the dealers were amateurs. They got it when they could afford it and sold it to friends and tourists, then went back to their day jobs. At larger quantities, those people moving hundreds of pounds were professionals. They were well financed, they knew what they were doing, and they made buckets of money. There was an unspoken professionalism of sorts with this group. They respected each other's boundaries, they didn't sell outside their territories, and if they did, they understood the consequences.

Charlie was new to the game and came into the big time without a real mentor or advisor to tell him how things worked. Angel's territory included the Keys, up to Key Largo, which seemed to have an understanding as a sort of no-man's land, several different dealers sold on Key Largo, and none of them got in the other's way. Anything north of the Keys was territory owned by the big dealers out of Miami. Stepping onto the mainland could be hard on a guy's health, but nobody ever told Charlie.

***

Jack had the shakes; he was hardly able to breathe and felt like he might puke at any second. Looking over the microphone, he saw Janie with a big smile on her face, and he felt a small wave of confidence rush through him. At her urging, he had agreed to do two songs at the Sunday open mic night at Mansion's Coffee House.

He stumbled through "Living till the Day I Die," forgetting some of the words and screwing up a chord or two. Yet the twelve people in the coffee shop, of which four were performers like himself, seemed to like it. Then he played "Laid Back and Key Wasted," which they really seemed to like.

Stepping off the tiny platform that functioned as a stage, he was hit with a wave of euphoric adrenaline as Janie rushed up and threw her arms around him. "You did great!" she said with a proud smile.

"I screwed up that first song, really screwed it up. But it was fun!"

"Nobody knew you messed up. You were fantastic," she said. "You have got to keep playing."

***

In the days since they had reconnected, Jack had been seeing more of Janie. Not dating as much as simply doing things together. He drove her up to Marathon where she bought a couple yards of fabric to recover an old chair that somebody had left for the garbage collectors, then he helped her with that project. One afternoon, she helped him polish the chrome on his boat. Jack was finding that beyond the booze and sex, Janie was smart, interesting, resourceful, and a lot of fun to be around.

On their second "real" date, Jack made her dinner, served on his front porch. He cooked a redfish he had caught and served it with rice and salad. They enjoyed a bottle of wine, he played her some old songs on his guitar, and when it was time for her to go, he gave her a single kiss goodnight and watched her walk away in the moonlight.

That night, he sat alone on his porch with his guitar and his yellow legal pad, and thought about all the events in his life that had brought him to be where he was at that moment in time. He thought about his job, and Ed, and Nancy, who he realized he had forgotten to call back. He thought about his decision to quit his job and drive south, he recalled the drive, and the wonderful scenes that had passed by his window as he drove southward.

Leaning over his guitar, he jotted down the words, "I loaded up my Jeep and stashed the top in the garage. I changed into my tropical attire. It was chilly through Virginia, but I hit the Outer Banks, and my attitude was toasty as a fire."

Viewing the trip south as a major turning point in his life, Jack played around with an upbeat tune to go with the words. He wrote the entire song in just over an hour. Actually, the song sort of wrote itself. When he was done, he played the entire song from beginning to end.

Finishing, he looked up to see if any of the neighborhood cats had stopped to listen. He was surprised to see the glow of a cigarette in the shadows of the porch next door. It faded away and was replaced with a puff of smoke that rolled out from under the roofline. "You got yourself a good song there, boy," he heard the old man say just before the hinges on the screen door creaked open.

Three nights later, at an open mic night hosted by Captain Tony's Saloon, with the same butterflies in his stomach and sweaty hands, Jack played "Southward" to his biggest audience ever, nearly thirty people. When he finished, they burst into applause, led by his favorite cheerleader, Janie.

Sitting at a little table with Janie, well after the last performer had finished, he played with his beer bottle, peeling the label off, trying to put it back on. "What's on your mind?" she asked.

"I don't know. I think we should get out of here, go somewhere less crazy."

Janie looked around the bar. It was pretty dead, virtually lifeless by Key West standards. “What’s less crazy than this?” she said while glancing around.

“I don’t mean this bar,” he said while rolling the base of his bottle around the table. “We should move somewhere less crazy.”

Was he kidding? she asked herself. They had slept together twice, been on two real dates, and did a few things together as friends. Was he really proposing they move away somewhere together? Uncertain of where he was headed with the conversation, she asked, “Where do you have in mind?”

“Have you ever been up to the Gulf Coast? My uncle used to live on Charlotte Harbor. I’d visit him as often as I could. It’s incredible up there.”

Janie looked at him like he had worms coming out of his ears. She took a deep breath, then let it out. Catching the attention of the waitress, she gave the international signal for another round, her pointer finger up in the air, spinning in a circular motion. This conversation was going to require a lot more alcohol.

“It’s a crazy idea,” Janie said to herself as she walked home alone in a bit of a daze. But crazy had pretty much become her norm since she had left Nevada a lifetime ago. She hardly knew the guy and she was still in a relationship with Greg. And what about that chick, Nancy? Janie asked herself if she was just a rebound relationship. Would Jack run to her like a faithful dog if Nancy showed up tomorrow?

CHAPTER ELEVEN

Charlotte Harbor

As if somebody had thrown a switch in Jack's brain, his focus had suddenly become Charlotte Harbor. He didn't know if it was an attempt to relive those carefree childhood summer days of fishing with his father and great-uncle, Red Carrol, or something much deeper, but the area was calling him and he was listening. He didn't know when or how, but as he had found his way to Key West, he knew he had to set a course for the Gulf Coast.

Lying in bed that night, he thought about his great-uncle Red, the best fisherman he ever had known. He remembered those magical days, the three of them fishing the salt flats of Florida, up and down the gulf. At his funeral, Jack raised a glass of rum and said, "The fish population in this part of the world has just breathed a reverent sigh of relief." Red was a crusty, yarn-spinning, truth-stretching, rum-swilling, masterful fishing guide and Jack had missed him every day since he had died.

The next morning, after a relatively sleepless night full of hopes and fears, Jack called his buddy Randy White on Pine Island. "Well, hell yeah, I can get you a job. Everybody's looking for good bartenders and I know several charters that might need a fishing guide. Did you ever consider using your college degree again?"

Jack laughed. He was convinced he had the whole damn thing figured out, but every time he spoke with an old friend, they would ask him when he was going to get serious about life again. They thought he was throwing his future away. "It's kind of hard being upwardly mobile when you're lying in the sun all day," one friend had told him. He put the line in one of his first songs.

"By the way," Randy said quietly before he hung up, "I heard they found a body in Shark River. It just might be our old friend, Charlie."

Jack cussed, then said, "I've got to get out of this town."

With some positive job prospects and Randy's offer of a place to stay for a few days, the only things holding him back were his boat and Janie. She hadn't seemed excited at all to join him on his pilgrimage to the north, and he was fairly convinced that she wasn't going to go with him. Somebody once told him that if you work for a large corporation, you could expect to be transferred shortly after you met the person of your dreams. It was a little-known law that Sir Isaac Newton stumbled across when he was tinkering with gravitation.

No corporations came into play, but the woman certainly did. For a moment, just a moment, Jack wondered if the sudden compulsion to move was a defense mechanism triggered by something deep in his brain. Running away from Janie before they got too close would prevent another heartache when he eventually screwed up the relationship. He dismissed the idea quickly; he didn't think even the most profound areas of his brain worked that way.

By noon, Jack had found a transporter to haul his boat to the greater Port Charlotte area, and the price wasn't horrible. Before dark, he had both engines running and the electrical system sort of patched back together. By promising them dinner, he talked two of the yard workers into moving the boat to the water and, for the first time since he had owned her, he saw the *Marauder* actually floating. His excitement overcame him, and he immediately forgot his promise of a meal and waved to the two as he idled out into the falling darkness on the maiden voyage of his first boat.

Jack's entire life had been centered around boats, yet he had never actually owned one. As a kid, his active imagination could take him anywhere. He sailed on a pirate ship, like every young man's dream. Across the southern oceans, he would sail his ship to distant islands for wonderful adventures with chests of gold. He grew up fishing on boats with his father and great-uncle. At age twelve, he started working on small, local charter boats as a mate. Three days after his eighteenth birthday, he had received his "6-pack" or charter captain's license, allowing him to take up to six paying passengers out, but always on somebody else's boat.

There was an indescribable feeling of pride that pulsated through him as he cleared the harbor and advanced the throttles. The two big Mercs behind him seemed eager to stretch their legs and show him what they were made of. Even Jack was surprised at the power and smoothness of the 225's.

He took her out around Fleming Key and up the cut between Sunset Key and Mallory Square. If he had enough fuel and beer, he would have gone all the way to Cuba, but lacking either, he took her out just beyond Fort Zackary before having to turn back for the docks. Easing her into an empty slip, he gave her a pat on the wheel. The impromptu shakedown cruise had gone flawlessly.

Walking home that night, all he could think about was boats, and fishing, and life. He didn't think about what he might be missing, or the time he had wasted hanging out on boats. He looked back fondly on a lifetime filled with boats, and how despite some troubled waters, he had always been able to stay afloat. He was as sure as anything the *Marauder* would be a big part of his future. Now he just had to work on that name.

***

Greg wasn't oblivious to the situation, Janie had become distant over the last several days. He had seen it before. As a younger man, he would have tried to find out what was bothering her or ask what he had done wrong. He would have stressed about losing her, lain awake trying to figure out how to keep her, paid extra attention, bought her flowers, and been grief-stricken when she left. But he was older and much more cynical than he had been in his youth. If she was leaving him, he would hold the door open and pat her on the ass as she walked out. Life was too short to get all wound up over a woman.

He liked her a lot, since she was an amazing woman. She was good at life, and she had a way of making strangers feel like old friends in minutes. And she was good for business. It was very rare for tourists to take two sunset cruises on the same trip to the Keys, but he noticed that when she connected with them, he was likely to see them aboard again in the next day or two. She had the right energy, the right personality, and the likeability to be successful in sales or politics. She stole the hearts of men and women alike, and he would be sad to see her go if that was what their sudden disconnect was about.

***

As he drove north five days later, Jack couldn't help but feel sad that Janie was staying behind. There was some connection there, a real and solid connection, different from anything he had ever experienced. They had enjoyed so little time together, he almost stayed. When it came time for him to go, they hugged, as neither was willing to let the other go. He finally told her to turn around and close her eyes, that he couldn't linger any more. "When you open your eyes, I promise I'll be gone," he told her. And when she did, he was.

He promised he would come back to see her, but he also knew what distance could do to even the strongest relationships, and he wondered how long it might be before that distance would make him fall for someone else.

Driving north towards the mainland was a different trip from his journey south all those months before. There wasn't a beautiful woman sitting next to him, and he wasn't appreciating the scenery nearly as much. Nancy had turned out badly, Janie had stayed behind, and after a few months, the beauty of the islands had become commonplace. But he was still excited. Heading for Charlotte Harbor felt like he was going home. It certainly had a more down-to-earth feel to it.

The Keys were a great place to visit, but seventy-five percent of the population was either transient or tourist, there for just a week or a month or two. Those who lived there on a permanent basis suffered from "Keys Disease." When the tarpon were running, few went to work. The rest of them were about half crazy. A popular line amongst the locals was "We're all here 'cause we ain't all there."

His time in the Keys hadn't been the escape to the tropical paradise that he had hoped. A lot of things had gone wrong, but it hadn't all been bad. In the next few days, his kickass boat would be following him north on a big trailer, he had met some wonderful people, and he had fallen in love with a dear old friend, his guitar.

Jack was on the road again, one of his favorite places, doing something he loved to do, heading for a new adventure. He had always had a wandering soul and a very inquiring mind. There was something down that open road that called to him whenever he got restless and felt the urge to roam. On Islamorada, he passed a family sitting on the tailgate of their station wagon, eating ice cream at a roadside café. It looked so ordinary to him, so different from his life. Some folks, he thought, like to hang right in the middle, most folks like to stay just where they are. But he liked to see what was down that highway, even though he knew that sometimes he took it just a little too far.

At Homestead, he had two choices. The fastest route was to take the turnpike to I-75. The other alternative was kicking over one block to South Krome Avenue and making a left turn onto SW 8th to the Tamiami Trail. That option would take much longer because of all the small towns, slower speed limits, and other distractions. Jack had always found that turning left, across traffic, led to some interesting adventures, so he turned left on the old road.

Driving through the Everglades at fifty miles-an-hour, he remembered family car trips along this very same road, everybody complaining about the heat and the boring, monotonous scenery. Jack couldn't be more content. His sweaty shirt stuck to the Jeep's vinyl seat, the sun roasted his forearms and thighs, but his hat shaded his head and the wind kept it pleasant. The Everglades had never been so beautiful to him.

Nearing the western bounds of the Everglades, he passed a sign pointing south to Chokoloskee Island. He remembered his Uncle Red talking about the ten thousand islands, saying some of the best fishing in the world was down that way. He turned around with a big grin on his face. His boss would understand if he was a day late getting to his new job, if he had a boss, or a job.

The beautiful blue-green and clear water on both sides of the causeway to Chokoloskee Island reminded Jack of the places he had fished further north, near the villages of Homosassa, Steinhatchee, and Sopchoppy. It looked like the fish were just waiting under the surface, ready to jump onto his line and into his boat with just a little coaxing from a lure or some live bait.

The island itself held a very typical, broken down, sun faded, weather beaten, Southern Florida village. It was at the end of the road, a gateway to nowhere and a place you had to want to go, not a place people would wander past on their way to somewhere else. Most of the buildings and homes were in need of at least a coat of paint, and many needed much more upkeep or repair. He drove slowly through the little town, slowing to let an old dog cross the road and swapping glances at a couple of school-aged boys standing near the road.

On the right side of the main street, Jack noticed a well-kept, bright coral building that seemed completely out of place, The Havana Café. Needing something to eat, a cool drink, and some local information, Jack pulled in.

As he walked up the three steps to the deck, he noticed to his right a beautiful patio area tucked in under a little grove of cypress trees. The umbrellas and a nice breeze made it look cool and inviting. Inside the café, he was impressed with the clean, open kitchen in the back. A woman working on something waved her arm, saying, "You're welcome to sit where you like."

Jack took the invitation seriously and headed for the wonderfully inviting patio where he found a shady table. The round tables and benches were poured concrete with incredible tile inlays; each was topped by coral fabric umbrellas and surrounded by a well-manicured garden of flowers. The pride of ownership was evident everywhere he looked.

The woman in the kitchen followed him after a few minutes with a menu and a glass of ice water. He ordered a beer and a blackened grouper sandwich without even looking at the menu. He would have been surprised if a place like this didn't serve grouper and even more surprised if they didn't serve it blackened. The woman gave a nod and left with the menu.

After a very short wait, a man appeared with his bottle of beer. He made a little show of wiping off the mouth of the open bottle with a fresh napkin before wrapping the napkin around the bottle to act as a koozie to help absorb the already forming sweat from the humidity.

"Welcome to the Havana Café," said the man. "Have you been to Chokoloskee before?"

"I haven't, but I wish I had. It's beautiful out here."

"Well, welcome. My name is Carlos. My wife Dulce and I own the café. Are you here to fish?"

"Perhaps," he said while reaching out to shake the man's muscular hand. "I'm Jack. How's the fishing been and are there any local guides on the island?"

Carlos gave a concerned look. "The fishing has been excellent. That's the problem. Our guides are probably booked up for weeks. But if you like, I'll check with Captain Corry to see if he has a spot in the next few days."

Jack told Carlos that he could go out the following morning, but if that wasn't available, he would have to go another time. He was excited to get to Pine Island. After a few minutes, Carlos returned with a second cold beer. He performed the same napkin ritual while telling Jack that he had spoken with Captain Corry. "He said it was not possible to go out tomorrow, and he didn't think any of the other captains would have room either, but I could check for you, if you like."

Jack thanked him; he said it wasn't necessary to check any further. "Tell me about your restaurant." Jack was truly curious about such a beautiful, well-kept café in such an out of the way place.

Carlos motioned to the concrete bench next to him. Jack nodded and the man sat down. "It's a funny story. I was a commercial fisherman all my life. But I loved to cook and dreamed of owning my own restaurant. One day, after years of dreaming, my wife and I decided to open this café. Whew!" he said with a look to the sky and a wave of his hand. "You should have heard my family. My mother-in-law said, 'Are you crazy? You've never run a restaurant, and you're going to open one here, in the middle of nowhere?' We could only smile and tell them it will all work out. And if it doesn't work out, at least we chased our dream. What's more important, I asked them, to live your life in a mundane world, or to take a chance and try to find your place in the few years we have on this earth?"

Jack blinked a couple of times and took a big swig of his beer. "I've been trying to find my dream. I'm chasing one now, but I don't really know exactly what my dream is or where I'm going to find it. Does that make sense?"

Carlos gave him a big smile. "It does to me, Jack. It does to me. Trust your instincts and do what you love. Hopefully, the happiness and money will follow." He stood up, patted Jack on the back, and said, "Enjoy your sandwich."

Driving north across the causeway off Chokoloskee Island, Jack heard the words over and over. "Trust your instincts and do what you love." He loved to fish, he loved to write songs and tell stories, and he thought if he could get beyond the nausea, the heart palpitations, and the sweaty hands, he would love to entertain people with his guitar. He imagined a life of fishing, writing, and singing his songs to crowds of people who were there to listen to his stories. That was his dream. Now he just had to find a way to make it happen.

***

Janie smiled when she saw Vido and Jodi walk into the Six Toed Cat for lunch. She hadn't seen them in several weeks. They were first-world refugees from corporate America. When she first met them, they told her they had come to the Keys several years earlier for a week's vacation. The next year, they quit their jobs and came down for the season, and they never went back.

They made ends meet by doing odd jobs. Vido could seemingly build or fix anything mechanical. Jodi was a wiz with computers; she stayed busy keeping the island online. They both held their charter captain licenses and sometimes disappeared for weeks while taking people sailing or ferrying a boat from here to there. They had led a fascinating life since their escape from the real world.

Vido and Jodi were some of the first people she'd met when she arrived on the island. They would disappear, then blow back into her life after a several weeks' absence and take up right where they left off. They were low maintenance friends, her favorite kind.

She delivered an order of shrimp and grits to table three, then raced over to give them each a big hug. "I'll get a sweet tea for me lady, and a cold Heineken for my lord," she said with a bow and her best English accent.

Jodi laughed and grabbed her by the forearm. "Oh, we've missed you, Janie. How have you been?"

"It's been an interesting few weeks," she said as the smile went away from her face. "I met a really great guy, dumped the other guy, and then watched the really great guy drive away as he moved out of town."

"Oh my gosh," Jodi said. "It sounds like we need some beach time together. Are you free after lunch?"

That made Janie smile as she thought about the wonderful friends she had made in her short time in the Keys. "We do, and I am."

***

Jack made the crawl north through Naples and Bonita Springs in what seemed to be the world's longest construction zone during rush hour. He thought the State of Florida must own every orange cone. In Fort Myers, he turned west and crossed the Caloosahatchee River on the Cape Coral Bridge, then traffic really started to slow down. He laughed to himself while waiting at a light behind an aging Buick driven by a small lady with white hair. HIs father once called Cape Coral "God's waiting room." He used to say, "You can get a table at any restaurant in town if you just wait until 6pm."

A few miles north, he turned left onto Pine Island Road. Stopping at a red light near the Publix, Jack noticed the strange street name of the crossroad. He had always been curious about street and road names and where they had originated. Some were evident, like Pine Island Road was obviously the road to the island, but the intersection he waited at was called Burnt Store Road. At some point, somewhere along the road, a store must have burnt. He'd have to ask somebody the story, if he remembered.

He drove past a large marina on his right and mangroves on his left, then out onto a little island where he passed some funky little joints that looked like they needed more research. One in particular, Bert's Bar and Grill, looked interesting to him. Before crossing the bridge to the little island of Matlacha, he saw a red sign near the Bridgewater Inn that stated "Island Time Starts Here."

He smiled, took in a big breath of the cool air coming off the water, then he took a little pressure off the gas pedal. He vowed to himself that from that point on, for the rest of his life, he would slow down, read more signs, and explore more cool bars. He was beginning to realize that life was too short to rush.

Randy was happy to see his old friend. They barbecued steaks and toasted their old buddy, Charlie. According to Randy's friend in the Monroe County Sheriff's Department, Charlie's death had been ruled an accidental drowning. There were no signs of struggle, but at the same time, it wasn't obvious how he got into the water. They found no unoccupied boats and nobody had reported an accident. "Sometimes we just find people floating around dead," his friend told him. Unless there was more evidence or conjecture to follow, the case was filed away.

"What ever happened to that sexy woman you were dating?" Randy asked, hoping to change the subject. "Did her temporary blindness finally go away?"

Jack laughed and admitted that Nancy had gotten smart. She had gone away and hooked up with a sailor. "I heard somebody say she was in Paris, and then Spain."

They drank and told stories late into the night. As Jack crawled into bed, his thoughts turned briefly to Nancy and then to Janie. The two women held no comparison to each other in terms of character. He could picture Janie standing on the beach in a warm ocean breeze, her hair blowing off her shoulders, her warm and sincere smile. Nancy would have complained about the no-see-ums, the mosquitos, and the wind and humidity messing up her hair and make-up. Jack would never see or talk to Nancy again, but for the rest of his life, he would think about her briefly every time he sang one of the two song he wrote about her.

***

Janie and Jodi sat in the garden behind the B&B. It was late, but a beautiful evening with a light breeze. The light clouds blew past the moon, almost around it, seeming to do their best to avoid obscuring the moon's view of the island. When the ladies were quiet, they could hear the light sounds of revelry coming from Duval Street a few blocks away. A Cuban Tree Frog croaked in the palms behind them, almost in unison to the snores of a guest up on the second floor.

They spent the evening talking about life, about relationships, about loves found and lost. Janie had never been in a relationship that lasted more than a few months. She had never taken them seriously because eventually the affair had to end so she could be with Bill. With that expectation now a thing of the past, she looked at dating in a new light. Greg had been a nice guy, but not "the guy." There was something, however, about Jack.

"So what are you going to do?" asked Jodi.

"What can I do? He left."

"You can go get him," said Jodi.

Janie pondered that idea for several long minutes while they sat in silence in the dark. The frog croaked, the guest snored, and a mix of music softly blew in from the bars to their south. "He knows where I am."

CHAPTER TWELVE

The Palm Tree Farm

Jack woke early. He fumbled around the kitchen until he found the coffee and filters so he could make a pot. He searched the cupboards until he found a large travel mug, and when the coffee was finished, he filled the mug and set out on a walk. The water was calling his name. A long and empty boat dock with a bench at the end looked inviting. Sitting motionless in the gaining daylight on his borrowed perch, he watched the day develop before his eyes.

Sanibel Island lay directly to his south. Off to his left, he could see the headlights of cars occasionally coming or going across the causeway. Just beyond that, the Sanibel Lighthouse still blinked its signal to ships and boats searching for safe passage to the ports at Cape Coral and Fort Myers. Ospreys, egrets, and pelicans arrived looking for breakfast. A pod of dolphins swam past, just a hundred yards off shore. Everything around him was beautiful, everything around him was a song.

Something about this place made him feel alive. He wanted to sing and play, he wanted to write. He wished he had brought his guitar and his yellow pad but knew if he left now to get them, he would return to a different, more mature day. He decided to stay right where he was, to soak it all up, and to try to remember the perfect morning that was unfolding before him.

The sun rising over the mainland to his left invaded the innocence of the incredible scene before him, but Jack was undeterred. He stood, smiled, and vowed to return. He loved the early morning. He just wished it came later in the day.

When he returned to Randy's house, there was a note next to the coffee maker that said, "Enjoy your day. I'll be back later. Randy." After helping himself to a couple of eggs and some toast, he took a quick shower, grabbed his guitar, and headed for his Jeep to go explore the island and the area.

He drove north up Pine Island to Bokeelia. Jack had no idea the island supported so many palm tree farms. He wondered if they were hiring. That seemed like a pretty good job. You plant a seed, lie back, and let Mother Nature do the hard part. He pulled to the side of the road and in the shade of the trees of a farm, he wrote, "Working at the Palm Tree Farm. The palm tree life sure suits me, it's the only way to go, plant a seed, sit back and watch 'em grow. There's something about those happy fronds waving in the breeze. Makes living seem so simple, and it puts my mind at ease."

At Bokeelia, he stopped in to Capt'n Con's Fish House to see if they were hiring. It looked like his kind of place, a salty dockside diner with a great view. "Good morning, bartender," he said as he took a seat at the bar.

The man behind the bar gave him a long look before guessing, "Red beer...no, Bloody Mary, extra spicy. Right?"

Jack gave him a nod. When the drink arrived, he said, "Do you know of anybody looking to hire a mediocre bartender?"

The man behind the bar laughed. "Mediocre would be an upgrade for this place. Too bad, we're not hiring at the moment. But things change quickly. If you want to fill out an application, I'll make sure the manager gets it."

Jack finished his drink, took the application, and tossed it in the trash can just outside the front door. He was after a job, not paperwork.

Driving south back down the island, he turned towards the mainland and crossed the Matlacha Pass Bridge. A car backed out of a parking space at Bert's Bar & Grill, causing him to slow down. He decided to take the vacant spot and check out the funky little bar. Fifteen minutes later, Jack had a job.

"Great!" said Jack. "When do I start?"

Bernard looked at the schedule for a moment. "Why don't you come in at four on Friday. I'll have you work with Brent Zepke. He's been here a long time, and he's a good guy to show you the ropes."

"That works for me," said Jack enthusiastically. "What day is today?"

***

Bert's was a tropical waterside dive, a once typical old Florida joint that was getting pretty rare to find. The developers had been buying up places like this and building condos for years. Some folks came for the music, some came for the view, some came to play in Matlacha and would stop in for a few beers.

Brent showed him around and gave him the ten-minute run down on how the bar operated, then he stepped in the back to replace a blown keg. Jack waited on his first customers, a nice couple who, when asked, said they were locals. Connie and Lamar Tench owned Useppa Charters. Lamar dropped his card on the bar.

"Well, damn," said Jack. "I just moved here. Do you know anybody looking for a fishing guide?"

Connie glanced at Lamar, who smiled. Before they left, Jack had his second job on Pine Island.

It turned out to be a relatively busy night at Bert's, even for a Friday. Brent told him the band, The Yard Dogs, usually brought in a pretty good crowd to hear their version of Swamp Rock, a blend of Cajun, zydeco, bluegrass, and rock and roll.

At the end of the night, after the band was done packing up their gear, and as Brent and Jack were getting ready to close, the band leader, Charlie Kuchler, plopped himself down on a stool at the bar and ordered a beer.

"Great show," said Jack. "That was fun to watch."

"Thanks, man."

Jack spun around and set a cold draft in front of him. "I play a little guitar. Do you know anywhere around here that does open mic nights or allows hacks like myself play for tips?"

"Yeah, there's a great little coffee shop in Punta Gorda called Perks. The owner is a guy named John Miller. Tell him I sent you, unless you're really bad. Then tell him Brent sent you."

Jack laughed, and Brent flipped Charlie the bird. "I'll just leave your name out of it from the get-go," Jack said to Charlie with a laugh.

***

Three days later, at ten in the morning, Jack was sitting on a barstool in front of a small coffee house crowd. The butterflies were still there, but his hands didn't sweat. He warmed up with a couple of cover songs, and a few people stopped talking and paid attention. He played "Laid Back and Key Wasted" and received a small applause when he was done. He played the song he had written on St. Simons, "I Just Came Here to Drink," and noticed a few people laughing at his lyrics.

He had planned to finish with "Southward," but when he completed the last chorus of "I Just Came Here to Drink," a lady at one of the front tables stood up and applauded. It was his first standing ovation ever, albeit just an ovation of one. He smiled and thanked her.

"I love your music," said the warm-faced, gray-haired lady. "But all of your songs seem to be about drinking. Don't you have a love song?"

Jack smiled. "I do have a love song. It's called 'Too Early for Drinking.'"

***

Jack's boat arrived in Fort Myers a few days later. He excitedly drove up to the marina to take delivery. Given the time of day, he only had time for a quick cruise down the Caloosahatchee River and across the sound to the island. He docked it at an empty slip close to Randy's boat just after sunset.

Waking up early the next day, he was very excited to finally have a chance to take his boat, which he had owned for a couple of months, out for more than a quick ride. He put a couple of sandwiches in a cooler full of beer and grabbed his guitar case.

At the marina, he filled both fuel tanks, then headed around the south point of Pine Island and pointed her north. Once he was out on Pine Island Sound, he opened her up. She felt like a race horse who had been given her head and seemed to leap across the long and low swells, bouncing playfully from one to the next. Captiva was on his left, Pine Island was on his right, and Cayo Costa, Cabbage Key, and Useppa lay ahead of him. He had never felt such incredible exhilaration or unbound freedom.

Captiva and Cayo Costa should have brought back bad memories of Ed and Nancy, but the memories just weren't there. Both islands were absolutely beautiful in the shining sun. At the northern end of Pine Island, he could see the Boca Grande Pass and the open ocean. As much as he wanted to, he decided to avoid going blue water until he felt a bit more confident in his boat. He smiled when he admitted to himself it wasn't the boat that concerned him, it was his mechanic skills that needed to prove themselves.

She was running well, so he ran up north and gobbled up the entire length of Boca Grande. The little town of Placida came into view ahead of him; he remembered it from his trips there as a kid and made a mental note that he needed to explore it again at some point. Running out of water at Placida, he turned her south and then east into Catfish Creek, where he slowed to an idle, then shut off the engines and enjoyed a cold beer while just floating on his boat.

It was quiet and wonderfully peaceful. He watched two osprey fish as wading birds darted here and there along a sandbar. The mangroves were green and lush, the water was blue and smooth; it was a beautiful setting. He lay back in the seat of the boat and looked up at the passing clouds, and slowly drifted off to sleep.

In his sleep, he heard a voice call out to him, saying, "Jack, it's so good to see you out here on the water today." He looked over the edge of the boat and up there near the mangroves was a talking manatee. He said, "You humans are crazy people, your land is full of highways, with buildings everywhere. Try to take life easy, take pleasure in every day. Try some grouper therapy, go sailing on the bay. Spend less time in traffic, don't go speeding everywhere. You humans are crazy people, you're much too busy way up there."

Jack awoke with a start. He looked out towards the mangroves, but there was no manatee and no voices. He was completely alone, just him and his crazy dreams, but he suddenly wished he wasn't.

Grabbing his yellow pad and a second beer, he wrote a quick letter to Janie, trying to describe the amazing scenery around him. He tried to set the incredible day he was witnessing into words on a piece of paper, but he knew he could never convey it accurately. He told her about his job at Bert's, he told her he was doing some guiding, and he told her about playing in the coffee shop to a rowdy group of senior citizens who seemed to have enjoyed his music. He told her he missed her and hoped to get back to Key West soon. Then he wrote that he was happy to be living where the sun was always shining, and if she ever got a wild hair, she was always welcome to come up and see him and his new life, living on the coast.

His beer was empty, his letter to her was complete, so he fired up the big Mercurys and blasted south towards an interesting splotch on the chart called Cayo Pelau. He anchored near a little mangrove island and fished a sandbar near Cape Haze, walking barefoot in the sand with his fly rod in hand for a few hours before heading up Gasparilla Sound towards Port Charlotte. The waters narrowed at Punta Gorda. He passed under the Tamiami Trail and I-75 bridges, then eased back on the throttles and took the north channel up the Peace River, following the outside bends in the river, hoping that was where he would find the deeper water.

Reaching into his cooler for a sandwich, he realized he had made a rookie mistake. The sandwiches had fallen into the melting ice and become soaked with water. They were both a soggy mess. Across the river, he saw a sign that read:

"Welcome to the Nav-A-Gator – You're Either Here or You're Lost!"

It sounded like his kind of place. As he eased up the channel, he could already smell the grilled onions and juicy burgers cooking on the grill.

Pirates of old found the same inlet a much different way. They followed a legendary 12-foot alligator, the Nav-A-Gator, which eventually became the namesake for the Old Florida bar and grill.

Tossing three bumpers over the side, he tied up to an old wooden dock and walked up towards the restaurant, happy to see the little backwoods place was open in the middle of the day.

As he walked towards the building, he could see it was, or had been, something more substantial than a backwater bar at a small marina. There was a decent-sized stage across the backyard from the low-roofed building. Picnic tables with green canvas umbrellas spread across the sandy yard held a few patrons here and there.

Walking in the back, the screen door slammed with an appropriate bang as he entered the refreshingly air-conditioned bar. The bar's walls were covered with somebody's crazy collection of stuffed fish, alligators, dollar bills, flags, and funny signs. It was unquestionably his kind of place.

He plopped himself down on a barstool, thinking, *I stopped by a bar in the middle of the day. That's kind of hard to believe*. When the lady behind the bar walking in his direction asked what she could get him, Jack replied, "I need four things. A Corona, a menu, a pen, and your name."

On his second shift at Bert's, a customer had asked his name and then used it frequently throughout the night. It was classy and appreciated. Jack decided he was always going to do the same when he was in bars or restaurants.

"I'm Christine," she said as she handed him a pen from her pocket. He quickly wrote down the lyrics about stopping by a bar in the middle of the day on a bar napkin. The random lines had been coming to him fast and furiously since he had moved. He wrote them on little scraps of paper, napkins, business cards, and stuffed them into his pocket.

Christine returned with a cold Corona and a menu. "Is this your first time at the Nav-A-Gator?"

"Yes, it is, but I bet it won't be my last. It looks like you guys do some live music here?"

"We sure do from time to time. We've had a lot of great musicians and bands play here. In fact, in about an hour, we have a guy named Yard Dog Charlie playing."

"I know Charlie!" said Jack.

At Christine's suggestion, he ordered a Super Grouper sandwich. She assured him that deep fried was the only way to go. He enjoyed his sandwich and another beer.

Yard Dog Charlie, as he was known when he played solo, arrived after a bit and warmly shook Jack's hand while congratulating him on finding one of the best bars in the area. Charlie asked about his gig at the Perks coffee house.

"It went okay. I didn't throw up and I didn't fall down," said Jack with a smile.

"That's a successful show in anybody's book," laughed Charlie.

Charlie played, Jack and a growing crowd listened. Jack got a bad case of the "one mores" and was finding it hard to leave. It was as if his barstool just wouldn't let him go. He jotted more lyrics on the back of the bar napkin from his pocket, then ordered another beer.

Sitting at the bar, he saw a girl across the room who reminded him of Janie. He wondered where she was and how she was doing. He thought back to an afternoon when they escaped a rainstorm at his little house near Smathers Beach. Good wine and conversation had kept them high and dry, and when they saw the sun again, three hours had passed in a blink.

Jack looked at the girl across the room and searched his brain, trying to remember Janie's face. It hadn't been long, but it was getting hazy, mixed in the big pile of memories hidden in the corners of his mind.

He had vanished from her life, never having been one to stay around. He wanted to see her again but worried that she might have also sailed away. It would just be his luck to hear that she too had found someone from Spain. He could really screw things up, he thought to himself.

Feeling sorry for himself, he decided it was time to go. As he stood, Yard Dog Charlie returned from the bathroom, "Jack, did you bring your guitar?"

"It's in the boat," he said.

"Well, go get it. Your soon-to-be fans are ready to hear a song."

Jack was just tipsy enough. He nodded to Charlie and headed for his boat.

***

Janie had been questioning her life over the last couple of weeks. What was she doing, where was she going, why was she here? None of those questions had mattered much to her since she had arrived, but something about meeting Jack again, and his leaving, had shook her up. Her time in the Keys had been exactly what she needed to gain some perspective on life, but now she was questioning where her life was taking her.

Working at the B&B and waitressing at the Six-Toed Cat had been fine, but she was starting to feel too old for that kind of life. She felt like a damn cliché.

Jodi and Vido were getting ready to ferry a big sailboat up north and had invited her to go along. Jodi agreed Janie needed to move on with her life, and they hoped a change in scenery would help. She hadn't turned down the invite, but she also hadn't agreed to go with them.

Janie had always been the strong one. She dated many men but had never let her guard down. Jack had been different. His words were magic, and he made her feel so good. It had been such a short time, they hadn't even had a real relationship, more of a casual friendship, but it had been something special. It was something she had never experienced before. Her heart hurt; it felt like something a crusty old salt of a fisherman had warned her about while showing her the crushers on a redfish. He told her, "It won't bleed, but it hurts real bad."

As she was finishing up and getting ready to close the Six Toed Cat at the end of the night, Jodi rushed into the restaurant. "Go grab your stuff, we're leaving tonight. There's a cold front coming down from the north and a tropical depression coming up from the south. Vido says if we leave tonight, we can skirt them both and be in Horseshoe Bay before they collide. Otherwise, we'll have to wait a week to deliver the boat."

Jodi seemed oblivious to the fact that Janie hadn't agreed to go with them. Janie started to argue but decided it was now or never. She left an apologetic note taped to the cash register for

Mark and Carla, the owners of the Cat, then rushed over to the B&B where she stuffed most of her belongings into a duffle bag and left a similar note for the Tighes. She felt horrible, knowing she was leaving both of them in a lurch with her sudden departure.

***

It was well after dark when Jack walked back down to his boat, his guitar case in hand and a big grin on his face. He had done a decent job of backing up Yard Dog Charlie and even played one of his own songs, with a little more confidence, and receiving a little more applause than his last show. He had met the owners of the Nav-A-Gator, Dennis and Nancy, and found a bar that made him feel like home. It was as if he was back on St. Simons. He carefully navigated his boat down the Peace River, then turned southward towards Pine Island Sound.

CHAPTER THIRTEEN

Night Watch

The *Watermark II* was a beautiful boat, an Eagle 54 with a large cockpit and a teak deck. Vido was waiting with the engine running when they got to the dock. Janie hardly had time to get her bag and herself aboard before he was tossing lines and backing out. She tossed her duffle on a bunk below, quickly glancing around the spacious saloon.

"Are we going to beat the storms?" she asked. Her sailing experience was limited to Greg's boat, always within sight of land, and the big booze cruise cat.

"We should be fine," said Vido. "Sorry for the sudden departure, but with the winds coming down almost directly from the north, we're going to have to run a hell of a long ways out into the gulf before we can tack back to Horseshoe Bay."

Janie wasn't sure what "a hell of a long ways" meant, but she was certain it was further out than she had ever been before.

An hour out of port, Vido set the watch assignments, giving Janie the first night watch. She shook her head. "I've never sailed before. I don't know anything about it."

"There's nothing to it. All you need to do is stay awake, listen to music, and keep an eye out for anything that we might hit that's bigger than we are. The auto-steer will do the rest."

He sat with her for a half hour, showing her how the automatic steering changed the boat's course slightly when the winds changed direction, always returning them to the northwesterly course he had set. They talked about other traffic, what the red, green, and white lights indicated on another vessel near them, and about which situations would require her to wake him up.

"Janie, in a noisy world, can you tell me what's more peaceful than the sound of the wind moving across the sail?" said Vido in a comforting voice. "When I'm sailing, it's amazing how I just leave everything behind. Relax, enjoy the journey."

When Vido felt comfortable with his new shipmate, he looked at his watch, told her what time he would be back to relieve her, and went below to join Jodi for some sleep.

Janie was almost in a panic for the first hour. She watched for dark ships to suddenly appear off their bow, she waited for the auto-steer to fail, she listened for whales surfacing in their course or the pow-pow-pow of attacking UFOs. After her first hour alone in the dark, she started to settle down. She discovered that she could tune in radio stations from Tampa, New Orleans, Houston, and even Havana.

She found a soft rock station out of Pensacola; the music and the rhythmic sound of the *Watermark II's* hull cutting through the long swells was relaxing, even soothing. She looked up, and the sky was a matter of amazement with a billion stars. They stretched from horizon to horizon, a 180-degree light show, unobstructed by buildings, or trees, or mountains. It was a hell of a light show, direct from the Milky Way. The world had such a different feel, alone beneath the stars. She had longed for a night like this. It was incredible.

She was just a sleepy sailor, on the night watch all alone. The boat rolled in the gentle waves and the rigging gently moaned. She put her back against the weather rail, and her mind was somewhere else. She had a million different and random thoughts, most of them centered around a guy who had left her standing alone on a street corner in Key West.

All those miles from landfall, carried by a fickle wind, without a soul in sight, she thought about her life. She had wanted freedom, to escape to someplace else. She had wanted to live and love on her own terms. Now she was in the middle of the Gulf of Mexico, she had a dollar in her pocket and a warm breeze in the sails, and they had a heading on the compass to a place she never seen.

There was a time, not long ago, when she longed for an ambiguous and uncertain future. But now she felt like she had grown through that stage of her life. She had survived the stormy days and she had stayed afloat. And even now, when she once again felt like she was picking up the pieces of her broken dreams, she believed she could weather any storm.

***

Arriving two hours early for his shift at Bert's, Jack confidently walked up to the stage, pulled his guitar out of its case, and stepped up on stage. He kicked a beer bottle left by the previous night's band and knocked over the microphone stand when he bent to pick it up. He gathered his wits, plugged in his guitar, gave it a strum, and then realized he had forgotten to turn on the amp.

The ten or twelve people scattered about the room looked at him with curious stares. He flipped a few switches, strummed his guitar again, turned a knob or two, said "Check, check" into the microphone, just like at real rock star, adjusted the volume again, and then turned back to the crowd.

He was going to explain who he was and what he was doing, especially to Bernard and Brent, who stood behind the bar with questioning looks on their faces, but he decided after such an auspicious entrance, he needed no introduction. He took a deep breath and stepped up to the mic. He played "Laid Back and Key Wasted," then "Southward," and "Livin' Till the Day I Die," all from memory. He was going to stop at three songs, but a pretty girl yelled out to him to play another. He reached into his guitar case and pulled out his big ol' yellow pad.

"This is one I've been working on, so I apologize in advance if I screw it up," he said to his little audience. "Growing up in Georgia, I had this neighbor who everybody called Old Man Tom. He was a great story teller, he would aggressively share the wisdom of his years, and if you promised not to tell your mom, he would even give you a swallow of his beer. I call this 'Old Man Tom', and it goes just-like-this."

He read the lyrics off his yellow pad while trying to remember the chords. He didn't play it too bad, and the crowd seemed to like it. He promised himself to massage it a bit more and add it to his growing repertoire. He gave his tiny audience a wave and packed up his yellow pad and guitar. Bernard shook his hand and told him he was welcome to play for free any time he wanted. That made Jack smile. Even Brent told him that he didn't suck, which coming from Brent was a compliment.

As Jack started his shift, he pointed towards a man sitting alone behind an empty bottle of Blue Moon. "Another?" The man nodded.

When he sat the beer before the man, he said, "I caught your show. I liked it."

Something about the way he strung out his words gave Jack pause. He replied, "But..."

He looked across the room in a moment of thought. "You're a good singer, and a talented guitar player, but you're a horrible salesman."

Jack gave him a quizzical look. "I'm not selling anything."

The man smiled. "You're selling every time you step up on the stage. If you're singing about escapism, and freedom, and sunshine, like your first song, you have to believe it. If you're taking us to an island or a beach, you need to get there first and guide us to you. Your product might be music, but if you want to be successful, you need to sell the dream of the ocean, living in a shack on the beach, a life without complications, without boredom or monotony, a life without stress. You have to learn how to make sunshine, warm breezes, rum drinks, and raw emotions ooze out of your speakers, and you have to do it in three minutes."

"That's a tall order," said Jack.

"It's like sex. If it was easy, everybody would be doing it." The man took a swig of his beer before adding, "I used to always play in my bare feet. Give it a try."

Jack wanted to talk to him more, but a couple at the other end of the bar wanted some Mai Tais. He made their drinks, then cleaned up the margarita the lady in the big yellow dress had spilled. When he returned, the man was gone. Under his empty beer bottle was a five-dollar bill and a single page of notebook paper, folded in half.

On the paper were the words and music to a song called "The Ballad of Coconut Pete." A note scribbled at the top of the pages said, "You're on your way. Take your audience on a beautiful trip every time you play. Don't be like Pete. Good Luck, Jim."

As Bernard walked past the bar, Jack caught his attention. "Hey, Bernard, do you know who the guy was sitting at the end of the bar?"

Bernard shrugged. "I don't know. Guess I didn't see him."

***

Janie woke and from her bunk listened to the sounds of the boat. They were different, not rhythmic like the night before. The roll of the boat had changed too. She got up, and after looking in the mirror and deciding there was nothing she could do with her hair, she pulled on a baseball cap and headed to the cockpit.

The skies had changed from clear to cloudy. The ocean wasn't blue but a foreboding shade of gray. Jodi and Vido were up on deck struggling with the luffing mainsail. The looks on their faces told her something was concerning to them.

"Do you need any help?" she asked over the wind.

"No," replied Jodi. "The main ripped out at a seam, just some piss poor workmanship."

"Can you fix it?" she asked.

"We can't fix it out here, but we can keep it from getting worse," said Vido. When they had finished what looked like a wrestling match against the sail and the wind, they both returned to the cockpit. Vido turned the boat and watched the now half mainsail fill with wind.

"Damn it," he said. "That's going to slow us down a whole bunch."

"What's your plan?" asked Jodi.

Vido rubbed the three-day growth of his beard while he thought through their options. "Well, with half a mainsail, there's no way we'll make Horseshoe before getting hit by one of the storms, and maybe both. And we sure as hell don't want to be out here in that crap with a patched together sail. I think we've got to make a run for Sarasota or St. Petersburg. Let's bring her about and head due east."

***

Jack had been enjoying fishing again. Lamar had been enjoying a little time off and was thrilled to be getting good feedback from his clients about his new guide.

After a trying day, Jack arrived at Bert's ten minutes late. He had been up before dawn to take a couple of boneheads from Idaho out fishing. After a day of tangled lines, bird's-nest reel disasters, and dealing with guys who were more interested in drinking than fishing, he got back home, jumped in the shower, and simply ran out of time.

Bernard, oddly enough, seemed happy to see him coming through the door at all. "Jack, geez, I thought you were going to flake out on me too. Did you happen to bring your guitar?"

Jack looked at him sideways. "Why would I have my guitar with me?"

"Well, go get it. You're on," said Bernard. "That jackass just called, his grandmother died...again. How many times can he use that excuse? How many grandmothers can one guy have?"

"I don't have enough to fill three hours," argued Jack.

"By the time you quit arguing and get your guitar, you'll only need to fill two. Now go get your guitar."

Jack was panicked and excited, all at the same time. He rushed home and rushed back. He did a fifteen-second sound check, then turned to face the crowded bar. He remembered everything the man with the melodic voice had told him. "Go to the beach, then bring the audience to you. Make sun and sand and rum drinks ooze from your speakers."

He kicked off his topsiders and stepped up to the microphone. "Good afternoon. I'm Jack, the, um, the bartender. But this afternoon, we're all going to pretend that I'm that guy with the cool guitar that you all came here to see...is it a deal?"

He took a deep breath and continued, "Some of my best years were spent on St. Simons Island up in Georgia. One day, my company transferred me to Wilmington, Delaware, and within days asked me to move to North Dakota. I quit my job, took the hardtop off my Jeep, tossed everything I owned into the back, and drove to the Keys. I have often regretted that decision. I sure miss that top when we get storms," he said while glancing towards the clouds rolling in.

The crowd laughed, and his confidence grew. "I wrote a little song about my life since I made that decision. I call it 'Laid Back and Key Wasted,' and it goes just-like-this."

He played every cover song he knew by heart and intermixed his own songs, including "Old Man Tom" and "Coconut Pete," the song he had learned from the mystery man at the bar.

The drunks from Idaho stumbled in, and the tall one yelled over the top of the music, "Hey look! It's Captain Jack playing the geetar!" An older couple got up and danced in front of the stage.

The guys from Idaho bought him a beer and when Teresa, one of the more "healthy" waitresses wearing a low-cut tank top, bent over to set it on the stage next to him, he said to the crowd, "You know, cleavage is like the sun. You can only look at it for a second. But if you're wearing sunglasses, you can look at it for a little bit longer."

The bar erupted in laughter. Teresa gave him a smile and blew him a kiss with one hand while pointing at her ass with the other.

In what seemed like minutes, the clock above the door indicated it was nearly time to end his show. "I have time for just one more. This is a song I wrote when I was living down in the Keys, and it's sort of become my personal anthem. A reminder to myself to not let life ever get in the way of living again. I call it 'Livin' Till The Day I Die.'"

Singing the last verse of the song, he looked out across the crowd and saw people paying attention to him, listening to his words and swaying to his music. He realized he was living his dream. He was playing his music at a little bar; he was making a living fishing, writing music, and playing his songs.

He strummed the last chord and received a rousing ovation. He was smiling from ear to ear when he saw her. His face went blank, and the crowd and the noise of the applause seemed to suddenly disappear. Janie was standing in the doorway.

"I can't believe you're here," he said, not realizing he was still standing two inches from a live microphone. The entire bar turned in unison to see an embarrassed Janie standing at the door. Jack set his guitar down, stepped off the stage, and rushed over to give her a hug, which prompted an "ahhh" from the audience.

Janie didn't know what to expect from Jack, and quite frankly, what to expect from herself when she saw him again. Her fears and doubts went away in an instant. He held her like he didn't want to ever let her go again.

"Damn, Jack. That was good!" said Bernard as he walked up to the two of them.

"Bernard, this is Janie," said Jack while still hanging on to her.

He shook her hand. "What did you think of your boy? He's in the wrong job. I've had him behind the bar. He needs to be behind the microphone."

Janie smiled and wiped a tear away. "I think so too."

Bernard gave Jack a chuck on the shoulder. "You kids get out of here. That storm's about to hit, which will chase away the crowd. Me and Loretta have this handled."

Standing there holding each other, Jack looked at her for a moment, then asked, "How did you get here?"

Janie looked down at his feet. "Where are your shoes?"

CHAPTER FOURTEEN

When the Sun Comes Shining Through

Randy was gone. He had flown up north to take care of some issues with his aging parents in North Carolina, so Jack had the house to himself.

It turned into a hell of a storm off the island. The chimes out on the back porch went berserk as the wind whipped up on the bay. The weatherman talked about a slow-moving tropical depression, stalled by a cold front from the north. When Jack and Janie saw the sun again, three days had passed them by.

When they emerged, they stepped into a new world. They walked the beach, hand in hand, in a world where anything was possible, a world where the sun shined a little brighter and the birds seemed to sing in harmony with the wind and the waves. They had each been in some dark and stormy places in their pasts, but the present day and their near future seemed bright and happy.

After breakfast at the marina, they spent a few hours working to clean up Jack's boat. They put together a picnic lunch and took the boat up to Useppa to a little beach on the south end that had been mostly protected from the storm. Jack anchored off the beach and they swam in, pulling the cooler behind them to their own little private oasis. After exploring the area for a bit, they sat together and enjoyed their lunch.

"If I asked you," said Jack after a long silence between them, "would you stay here with me?"

Janie laughed hard enough that she snorted. She turned and gave him a little punch in the shoulder. "I wasn't going to wait for you to ask. I made that decision three days ago."

They spent the next day searching for a little place of their own. The rents on Pine Island were horribly expensive, so they were forced to look on the mainland. Neither one of them liked the size or feel of Fort Myers or Cape Coral, but a smaller town just to the north held promise.

They drove up to Punta Gorda and found a furnished, fifties era house on Carmalita Street. Jack paid the deposit, they signed the lease, and the next night, after his shift at Bert's, he drove "home" to find Janie waiting for him with a late-night candlelight dinner and a bottle of wine.

Jack didn't care that he had to get up early and drive back to Pine Island for a fishing charter; he was happy, Janie was happy, and that was all that mattered at that moment in time.

***

A few days later, Janie interviewed for and shortly after was offered a job in human resources at the Charlotte County School System. Jack took a bartending job at a cool bar called the Ice House Pub just a few blocks from their home. He took another as a fishing guide with Captain Billy out of Punta Gorda.

Bernard hired Jack to play Wednesday afternoons at the bar, which luckily, he was able to juggle into his other schedules. When he found time, Jack liked to play at the local coffee shops and bookstores. He found several who were thrilled that he would show up and play for tips. Jack was happy to have the opportunity to play to a group of people that were there to listen. Often at Bert's, he was simply background music to the patrons who were there to drink and talk.

At the smaller venues, he could try out his new songs. He was able to see the reactions on the audience's faces, he could judge the impact of his music. He found that, through his songs, he could make them laugh, he could make them ponder, or even remember a love from their past. He learned that he could get them smiling or laughing at one song and bring a tear to the corner of their eyes with the next.

After dinner one night, Jack and Janie sat together out on their tiny screened-in porch enjoying a couple of rum drinks. Jack lightly strummed on his guitar as they talked about each of their days and plans for the coming week. That led to a conversation about the future, and the past, and eventually about them.

"Are you ever going to leave me again?" asked Janie after a long silence.

Jack continued to strum his guitar and then sang her a line he had been massaging for a while. "I'll be here till the light dies in your eyes."

She smiled and laid her head on his shoulder. For now, that was good enough.

***

The next morning, they drove down to Pine Island. Janie drove the Jeep back to Punta Gorda while Jack brought the boat up. Richard Wilson, a nice old retired guy who frequented the bar, had a home with a dock and a boat lift that he wasn't using in Bal Harbour. He said he would swap Jack use of his dock and lift for his favorite kind of beer, free and cold. It was a great deal for Jack—slide a few drafts across the bar and he'd have a dock within walking distance of his house.

Richard had also told him about a good yet inexpensive boat mechanic at a little place up the river. The *Marauder* was still in need of some electrical work and a new name. Meeting back in Punta Gorda, Jack and Janie headed up the river, following sketchy directions given to him by a drunk in a bar, to find some guy named Eddie at a little marina.

Finding Eddie was easy enough. He worked at a little broken down, nameless marina. The sign pole that once held a Marlboro sign with the marina's name below had been blown over in a storm, years and years earlier. The marina had been there long enough that everybody knew where it was. The owner never got around to replacing the sign and eventually the pole was used to prop up part of the dock.

Over the years, very nice, large homes had been built up and down the riverbank on both sides of the marina. It now stuck out like a sore thumb, oddly out of place even though it had been there for fifty years before the homes were built.

Jack eased up to the dock, kicked two fenders over, and tied up. A man wearing a greasy t-shirt and a Red Sox cap slowly walked over while wiping his hands on a dirty grease rag.

"I'm looking for Eddie," said Jack.

"Ya found him."

"Richard Wilson said you were the best. He said you could help me finish up a couple of things on my boat."

Eddie shook his head. "I'll sure give it a try. Whatda need done?"

Eddie was just about as red as rednecks could get in this part of the world. He had grown up a few miles inland, further up the Peace River, and learned to work on boats alongside his dad at an early age. School really hadn't been his strong point. He flunked out of high school in his junior year. While his classmates were going to the prom, Eddie was working on boats. After they came back from college to become doctors and lawyers, he worked on their boats.

He and his girlfriend lived on a derelict schooner that had been abandoned at the marina after the owner died. When Eddie finished fixing her up, the mechanics were top notch, but she looked like hell and leaked in so many places that he had never been able to find them all. It didn't matter to either of them. They anchored up in the back bays where they could live for free, not having to pay moorage. They lived on love and rum and were happy as they could be.

Jack showed him the projects he needed help with, mostly the electrical system, but he also wanted him to do some fine tuning on the engines.

"I can help you with all of it," said Eddie. "But I won't be able to get to it for a few days. I gotta finish up an engine rebuild, and Saturday, I'm getting married."

Janie perked up. "You're getting married? Congratulations! What's your fiancée's name?"

Eddie sort of blushed. "I'm getting married to my Pearl."

"That's so cool," said Janie. "Where are you getting married?"

"It'll be on the beach at Ponce de Leon Park, seven o'clock, everybody's invited. We'll have a keg of beer."

"We'd love to be there. We'll try to make it," said Janie with a big smile.

Jack shot her a look. What in the hell was she talking about?

Eddie and Jack shook hands, and Jack said he'd bring the boat back on Tuesday. As they eased away from the dock, he looked at Janie. "Why would you tell him we'd come to his wedding?"

"He seemed like a nice guy and we don't know anybody here. It'll be fun."

Jack rolled his eyes. A redneck beach wedding with a keg of beer. Fun wasn't how he would describe it, but it would certainly be interesting. "How about some lunch?" he asked. "I found this cool little place up the river a while back. I want to talk with the owners about possibly playing there."

"Sure!" said Janie as she leaned back and put her feet up on the console. She looked over at her handsome boyfriend at the wheel of his boat. With the river and the green bank behind him, his sunglasses, and the wind blowing through his hair, he looked like a movie star. Or at least he did to her. She was pretty happy with her decision to move north.

Janie had her doubts as they walked up to the backdoor of the Nav-A-Gator. Jack's "cool little place" wasn't what she had envisioned. She kept an open mind and was pleasantly surprised at the great little bar. Susy brought them a couple of beers, a Nav-A-Gator pilsner, which they both agreed was tasty. They feasted on alligator bites and then shared the fish and chips.

Jack recognized Nancy, the owner, standing at the end of the bar looking over some paperwork. He excused himself to go talk with her. "Hi, Nancy, my name is Jack. We met a while ago, the first time I came in. I played a few songs with Yard Dog Charlie, but I'm not sure if you were still around."

Nancy made a good show of acting like she recognized him, but a lot of people came through the bar. Jack told her, "I'm a singer/songwriter, I'd like to see if I could get on your schedule and play here from time to time, maybe even call this my home bar."

She smiled at him. "We'd love to have more live music, but I'd like to hear you perform before we commit to anything."

Jack reached into his pocket and pulled out a cassette tape. "I don't have my guitar with me today, but I brought one of my songs for you to hear." Nancy took it from him, saying she would have a listen in a bit when she finished her project. Jack returned to Janie and ordered two more beers.

"How did that go?" asked Janie.

"She said she would listen to my tape," he said with a shrug. "I wrote my name and number on it. I guess we'll see how it goes."

They visited with two fishermen sitting next to them while they finished their beers. Janie grabbed Jack's arm as his voice wafted across the bar singing "Laid Back and Key Wasted." Five minutes later, Jack was on the schedule to play the following Thursday afternoon at the Nav-A-Gator.

When Saturday rolled around, despite his hopes that she would have forgotten, Janie dragged Jack down to the wedding of Eddie and Pearl. Jack thought Eddie was the ultimate redneck, but he was a candidate for Mister GQ when compared to some of the other guests. The crowd of about fifty people was amazingly diverse. Some looked as though they had just crawled out of the swamp while others appeared to be quite wealthy, perhaps some of the yacht owners who knew of Eddie's talents.

Their chapel was simple, a couple of dozen mismatched beach chairs, a folding table for cards and gifts, and a garbage can containing an iced keg of beer. Their backdrop was Charlotte Harbor and the setting sun. Jack and Janie stopped and gazed out over the water; it truly was an impressive cathedral.

Eddie cleaned up good. He wore a tropical shirt and a new pair of cargo shorts. He proudly introduced "his Pearl" to Jack and Janie and then pointed them towards the keg. The wedding plan was simple. It was a party on the beach, which at some point would be interrupted long enough so Pearl and Eddie could get hitched.

The adults stood around drinking beer, the kids ran and played and waded in the bay. One of the mothers filled her toddler's baby bottle with Pepsi as a lady in an expensive dress, who refused to take off her high heels on the beach, looked on in disgust. Jack took notes as quickly as he could. Some of the things he saw and heard, he just couldn't make up.

Pearl told them that she and Eddie had met one night down at the Our Place Tavern. They were swapping shots and must have had a bunch because they ended up leaving together. She laughed, saying that he was looking for a one-night stand, but she had at least a three-night minimum. "Now," she told them, "it looks like we might be together for years. We'll see."

She was the daughter of a Baptist preacher who went to jail when the cops found the dope. Her mom was killed in a bar fight.

Eddie didn't seem to have much of a future and Pearl had a lot of past, but they were happy and in love.

As the sun began to set, a tall, heavy set bald man with a long beard, dressed in shorts and a Dodge Ram t-shirt, called everybody together around the keg. "I'm Ed Earl, Eddie's cousin, on his mama's side," he told the crowd. "When Eddie told me he and Pearl were getting married, he asked if I'd do the honors. So, if I can get y'all to pay attention for a few minutes, and somebody to hold my beer, we'll make these two legit."

The entire ceremony lasted less than five minutes, and everybody cheered when the barefoot couple exchanged their vows. Ed Earl announced them as man and wife and somebody handed them fresh beers so the small crowd could toast them and their tenuous future.

As they walked back towards the parking lot, hand in hand, Janie said, "Now that was a nice wedding."

Jack smiled and sarcastically said, "We ought to have the happy couple over for dinner one night." Janie punched him in the shoulder.

***

The days stretched into weeks and the weeks into months. Janie was enjoying her job; it gave her a sense of consistency that she missed while living on the island. She had lived the life of a drifter, and she had enjoyed her time in Key West. It had changed the way she would view the rest of her life, but now she appreciated a sense of stability. She fully supported Jack and his less than conventional lifestyle, and when she could, she loved sitting in the audience and watching him play.

Jack was taking tourists fishing, bartending at the Ice House, and playing regular gigs at Bert's and the Nav-A-Gator. In his spare time, he still loved to play at a coffee house or local bookstore for free. His fan base kept growing.

His small but enthusiastic group of fans continued asking him for three things. They wanted him to develop a website so they could keep up with his schedule, they wanted him to release a CD, and they wanted to hear more original songs.

Building a website and producing a CD were so far outside his scope of knowledge that it was easy to put them off. He told his fans that he was working on both, but beyond some brief research, he hadn't started either project.

New songs were coming to him from every direction. It seemed like the more he wrote, the more he saw. The world around him was filled with ideas. Fishing trips, drunks in bars, a walk on the beach with Janie, all of them seemed to contain ideas for songs. He wrote them down on slips of paper and stuffed them in his pocket. When he got home, he put the scraps of paper, bar napkins, and random business cards in a drawer and when he needed a line for a song or a new song altogether, he sifted through his idea drawer.

Looking through the drawer was always hilarious. On the back of a receipt might be a phone number but no name. On a post-it note, he would find a name, such as Ed Cunningham, but no clue as to why he wrote it down. Other scraps held lines, some brilliant, some really bad. "I'm off the coast of Scotland, in a fiberglass canoe, on my way to Iceland, to put the moves on you." He made a mental note to himself to one day do something meaningful with all the nonsense in his drawer.

When he had a few hours alone, he would jump into his boat and head to some of his favorite fishing spots off Cayo Costa or Boca Grande. He loved to fish but spending time alone, stretched out on his boat, drifting where the breeze wanted him to go was his favorite activity. Watching the clouds drift by seemed to recharge his batteries, both physically and creatively. He wrote some of his best songs either sitting on his boat or staked out on a remote beach somewhere.

After finishing up a set at the Nav-A-Gator one afternoon, a guy he had known around the bar for a long time walked up to the stage. "Jack, we're taking my new party barge out tomorrow night for a big beach party. It's a full moon," said Mark. "You and Janie need to come along, everybody's going: Dennis and Nancy, Bob, Crazy Mark and his wife. Pack up some food, bring your guitar, and meet us at the dock around seven." It sounded fun to him. He looked over at Janie, who enthusiastically said yes.

Arriving at the dock, Jack and Janie quickly realized they were running with a crazy crowd. Mark brought a case of Patron, Bob dressed like he wanted to be gay, and as they pulled away from the dock, they found out that the plan was to stay until dawn, or at least until the liquor was gone. They motored towards the sunset with Mark proudly at the helm of his new vessel, drinks were flowing, and everybody was in a party mood. After forty minutes, Mark eased the nose of the party barge up on a beach of a little island out in the sound.

Wally unloaded a generator to power a small sound system that Jack brought along, and within minutes, they had a fire going and Jack was playing his music loud while the small group sang along. Dennis came out of the dark wearing a skimpy thong. Nancy begged him to put his clothes back on, but nobody cared.

They pulled food and booze out their coolers. Janie's deviled eggs, a recipe from her grandmother, really went over big. The shrimp started boiling when the water got hot and the cold drinks kept flowing. Alex fell asleep when he ran out of gas, Coach got drunk and started screaming like a banshee and then turned and mooned the crowd, but nobody cared. They just laughed at his antics.

Jack took a break from playing and Wally hooked a CD player up to the sound system. They all danced in the sand to their favorite songs. After a while, Janie found Jack sitting at the edge of the fire's light writing on his yellow pad. "Whatcha doing?" she asked.

"I'm turning this night into a story," he said with a smile. Then he looked up towards her and wrote down the line "Turning nights into stories."

They partied through the night and toasted the sun as it started to rise. After packing everything back on the boat, they did a quick head count, which came up one short. A quick search found Dennis sleeping in the spurge grass, covered in mosquito bites. Heading back, they all decided it had been one hell of a night and on the next full moon they were going to do it again.

CHAPTER FIFTEEN

I Don't Know Where I Am

One advantage of playing in Southern Florida as opposed to, say, Cleveland, was that half of Jack's audience were tourists from elsewhere. As he started to gain popularity with the locals, he also made fans from other areas. He was excited to be hired to play a backyard party in Pensacola, but he was elated when he was invited to play a last-minute show at Meeting of the Minds, an annual quasi Jimmy Buffett festival in Key West.

He quickly assembled a couple of guys he had met along the way: John on steel drums, Jimi on guitar, and Doc Martini on the drums. They practiced two and a half times at the Nav-A-Gator. The third practice was cut short when a couple who was listening started buying them drinks. That started another night that would eventually become another story.

Because of other commitments and a flat tire, they arrived in Key West just forty-five minutes before they were to go on. The show was a three o'clock start at the Oak Beach Inn, an outdoor venue at the far reaches of the tourist section of Duval Street. They started playing to a "crowd" of six people who had wandered past and had stopped by for a quiet mid-afternoon drink. By the end of their first set, the crowd had nearly doubled in size, Jack counted eleven, if you included the drunk sleeping at the back table, and the toe-tapping waitress.

As they started their second set, the original three couples paid their tab and left. Jack told the band to play like there were forty thousand screaming fans in the arena, and they did. When they finished their second set, the bar was nearly full; unfortunately, it was full of people getting seats for the next band, a Jimmy Buffett cover band.

As they started to pack up to leave, Jack tried to think up a pep talk for his "team." They had driven six hours to make a couple of hundred bucks for playing to a tiny crowd. It was hardly a win.

A middle-aged, confident-looking man with slicked-back hair approached Jack. "I love your music. I get so tired of Buffett song after Buffett song, cover after cover. Who writes your music?"

Jack thanked him, and then told him he had written all the songs they played except for a Jerry Jeff Walker cover.

Hearing that, the man almost couldn't get his business card out fast enough. "I'm Michael Heeb with Wilshire Records. Can I buy you dinner?"

The guys went out on the town to hear music and flirt with pretty women, as Jack and his newly found friend went to The Commodore's Boathouse for dinner.

"Our group looks for promising new artists like yourself and we give them the direction to become big," said Michael over his cocktail. "Once we sign you, we take all the nasty work out of your way. We help guide you to success, we help you with your song selection, we set up your tours, we produce and sell your CDs, manage your website, set you up with a great backup band, handle all the negotiations and accounting. We get you in the right venues and on the right radio stations to build your fan base quickly. We basically take over so all you have to do is write your music and sing your songs."

That all sounded good to Jack. Heeb was talking about handling all the pieces and parts of the business that Jack didn't really want to or know how to do himself. "You must get a pretty healthy cut of revenues to do all that."

"Of course we do, but you need to look at it like this. If you did it all on your own, and if you were very successful, you might end up making forty or fifty thousand a year. We help push you to the top, your revenue goes through the roof, and if you're moderately successful, you'll make two or three hundred thousand a year. And we do all the work."

Jack couldn't believe that he was sitting in a nice restaurant being courted by a record executive. He reminded himself that Heeb was with a record company out of Atlanta that he had never heard of, but he still couldn't wait to call Janie and tell her.

"What's the next step?" asked Jack.

"We'll get you up to Atlanta where the bigwigs can hear you play, chat about your goals, talk about our expectations, and then if it all fits well, we sign you up and kick your career into high gear."

It all seemed to be happening. Jack enjoyed a delicious yellowtail snapper and they shared an expensive bottle of Cabernet Sauvignon, all paid for by his new best friend. After dinner, they walked along the marina. Michael asked him which of the large yachts he planned to own in a year.

Passing by Schooner Wharf Bar, somebody yelled out, "Jack!" Jimi and John stumbled out of the bar. "Jack, we've been looking all over for you!" John said excitedly. "Schooner's had a cancelation, and they need a band to play tomorrow at seven. We told them we're in!"

Jack was excited, but they hadn't planned to stay two nights. He hoped the money was good enough to pay for another hotel night. After he thought about it for a moment, none of the money or logistics mattered. They were playing Schooner's, in the heart of the festival and at seven o'clock. The crowd would be huge.

Heeb pulled him to the side, away from the guys. "Jack, I don't think playing tomorrow is a good idea. You're on the edge of something big. You need to start thinking big, not playing these little venues with a pieced-together band."

Jack laughed and jokingly said, "Ah, hell, Michael. You're just afraid some other agent or record company will see us and try to sign us." It was the furthest thing from Jack's mind, but something in the look that Michael gave him told him he had hit the nail on the head. Everything Michael had said to him suddenly took on a different light. He had said they would help him with his song selection, find him a backup band, set up his tours, and produce his CDs. In other words, they would tell him what to play, who to play it with, and where to play it.

Finding Evalena, the manager of Schooner Wharf, Jack agreed to play for a couple of hundred bucks, and they sealed the deal with a handshake. Jack got the feeling that there was no way he was going to shake Michael, so he told the guys to meet him at the Hog's Breath Saloon. He found a group of pretty girls standing around a table and introduced himself to a hot brunette. He shook her hand, palming her a neatly folded twenty-dollar bill, and whispered in her ear, "Can you keep my buddy occupied for five minutes while I sneak out the back?"

She laughed and said back, "Heck, we'll keep him busy for ten minutes if you're buying the drinks."

Jack told Michael that he had to hit the men's room, and ten minutes later was buying his guys a round at the Hog's Breath Saloon while they watched a great band play.

After the Hog's Breath, they made the crawl down Duval Street, hitting all of Jack's favorite bars along the way: Sloppy Joe's, Captain Tony's, and Rick's. They stumbled over to the Green Parrot, where Jack ran into some of his old "associates" from his smuggling days, and then down to Murphy's where his bartender buddy, Busch, was so happy to see him that he bought Jack and the guys a round of drinks.

Sometime around four in the morning, as they were trying to find their way back to their hotel, they came across a very attractive woman suffering from an acute intestinal malady, not uncommon in Key West at that hour of the morning. Her boyfriend or husband was rubbing her back and giving her words of encouragement as Jack and the guys walked past.

The man looked up and made eye contact with Jack, and the words "She's a beauty, but she's got rabies" popped into Jack's head and out of his mouth. The guy made a suggestion about something obscene Jack should do to his mother.

Jack laughed at himself and kept walking, saying to his buddies, "The things you do when you're drinking, they seem to make so much sense."

Waking just after noon, Jack attributed his hangover to the cost of research. If he was going to be the guy who sang about beaches and booze and women, he had to be engaged in constant, cutting edge research. He sat up in bed and then lay back down, thinking he may have done too much research the night before. Two hours and a couple of beers later, Jack was sitting by the pool feeling pretty good. Jimi and John found him poolside and joined him.

Nobody had seen Doc since; well, they couldn't remember what time of night Doc had disappeared, but they were able to narrow it down to sometime between sunset and four in the morning. Jack offered up a toast to him. "Last night was a suicide mission from the very beginning. The odds were stacked against us, mistakes were made, good men were lost. Here's to Doc." They raised their glasses to their fallen comrade.

Five minutes later, Doc arrived poolside. When Jack asked him where he had been since they saw him last, he just grinned and said, "It's complicated."

When they arrived at Schooner's to prepare for their big show, they noticed the schedule showed the band playing at seven o'clock as "Jack and The Fish Heads."

"Who came up with that name?" asked Jack.

Jimi laughed. "When we found out they were desperate for a band, we told them we were kind of a big deal and we'd be happy to step in. They asked our name, and since we hadn't talked about it, that's what I came up with in a couple of seconds."

Jack twisted his head, picked up an amp, and said, "Works for me."

Michael Heeb was there. "Jack! I lost you guys last night. I was doing really well with that pretty brunette, and then all of a sudden, she went from hot to cold. I looked around, but you guys had all disappeared."

"Yeah, we didn't want to get in the way of a master engaged in the art of wooing a woman, so we quietly snuck out," said Jack with a smirk. "Sorry to hear it didn't work out."

"Luckily, the beer here is as cold as she was," he said with a grin. "Hey, Jack, I brought a Letter of Intent for you to sign," said Michael as he pulled a piece of paper out of his briefcase. "It develops an understanding between us, and it starts the ball rolling towards your first million dollars."

Taking it from him, Jack said, "Thanks, Michael. I'll take a look at it over the next couple of days and then we can chat some more."

"It doesn't tie you into anything; it just starts our relationship and your brilliant career with Wilshire Records. If you sign it now, you won't have to get it to me later. I'll give you a copy of it to review when you have a chance. We're all about making your life easier while making you wealthy."

Jack smiled and pointed to a heavy speaker. "Grab that and follow me."

By seven, the Schooner Wharf Bar was packed. Jack felt the old familiar butterflies returning. He had never played to a crowd this big. He turned to his band and said, "Okay, guys, let's pretend we're real rock stars. Keep it tight, play with confidence, and they'll never know the difference."

They opened with "Laid Back and Key Wasted" and then went to "The Ballad of Coconut Pete." They played through the first set and ended with huge applause. Michael was in the front row, his contract and pen sitting on the table next to his drink.

A large woman approached the stage between sets, a twenty-dollar bill in her hand. "I want to buy your album."

Jack lied, "It's coming out soon. Leave us your name and address and we'll get you one."

During the second set, people danced next to the stage and stuffed money in the tip jar. A guy from Oklahoma bought the band a round of beer, a couple from Maryland bought them a round of shots. A drunk girl with a perfect set of breasts flashed the band. The owners were happy; they were making a haul.

"Thanks, everybody, we've had a really great time tonight," said Jack as their time wound down. "We've played a few songs, witnessed some crazy body movements that were either supposed to be some form of dance or a satanic ritual, and we saw more of a pretty girl than we ever thought we would while on stage." Jack laughed as the girl stood and flashed them again. "You just cannot un-see that!" he said to the roar of the crowd.

"A little over a year ago, my girlfriend Janie decided to quit her corporate job. She completely changed her life, tossed away everything she knew, and drove down to the Keys. It turned out to be a good thing, because that's where we met for the second time. I wrote this last song about her trip. It's called 'Mary Jane Goes to Key West,' and it goes just-like-this."

Near the back of the restaurant in a dark corner, a beautiful, classy woman with an incredible body, the kind of woman you wouldn't normally see in a place like Schooner's, stood and silently walked out of the bar. Several men stared and wondered who she was.

When they finished, the crowd was on their feet wanting more. Jack couldn't believe it. He blushed and waved them off while making two mental notes: one was to produce a CD as quickly as possible, the second was to always keep a song in reserve for an encore. His little band had played every song they knew.

As they started to break down their gear, people made their way to the stage. A man shoved his card at Jack, saying, "You've got to come play in Omaha. My buddy has a great little beach bar there. You'd fit right in."

Some nasty old lady tried to pick him up. She slipped him a bar napkin with her name and room number on it, and a guy from Charleston wanted Jack to play at his annual summer bash out by the lake. Wendy from Seattle wanted to know how they could get them to play out there soon, and the president of the Bozeman Parrothead Club had to get Jack's phone number so they could put a show together.

High on adrenaline, loading their equipment in the back of the van was an easy task. They ditched Heeb after everything was packed up. They all agreed he was a nice enough guy, just a bit too aggressive. The four of them floated a foot above the ground as they walked over to Mr. Z's for a cheesesteak. As usual, it was way too stinking hot when it was delivered and they could barely eat it.

On Duval Street, they tried every drink and every bar. They saw some great bands and did some dubious stuff that they would later barely recall. At quarter to three, somebody suggested shots of Wild Turkey at Tony's, which seemed to make sense.

From a pay phone on the corner, Jack called and woke up Janie. Given the hour, and that she could tell from his first words that he was absolutely blasted, she was very patient with him. He excitedly told her about the show, the crowd, the people who wanted to buy CDs, the people who wanted him to play in towns with names he couldn't remember. He admitted he had partied too long and drank way too much. She told him he needed to get back to his room and get some sleep. He told her he was in a bit of a jam, because "I don't know where I am."

Janie asked him to put Jimi on the phone. Jimi said, "Don't worry, I got this. I'll get your boy to his room."

She smiled and laughed as she hung up the phone and laid her head back on the pillow. It must have been one hell of a show.

The drive back up to Punta Gorda was miserable. John was able to drive most of it. He traded off with Doc for the last hour and fell asleep in the back of the van. Jack again swore he would never drink again. They dropped him at his house and he slept until Janie came home from work. She sat on the edge of the bed and stroked her fingers through his hair to wake him up gently.

"Hey," said Jack quietly.

"Are you going to survive?" she asked with a smile.

"They're giving me a 50/50 chance, which is better odds than I had a few hours ago."

On the table next to the bed was a pile of credit card receipts, and slips of random paper with names, phone numbers, and lyrics written on them. Janie glanced through them and found a bar napkin with "Linda, Ocean Key Resort, Room 217" written on it.

"I see you really impressed Linda," she commented.

"Who?" Jack asked without opening his eyes.

On a slip of paper, he had written, "I started out last night with good intentions, but I ended up getting sideways drinking wine. The last thing I remember we were roaring, till something hit my head and knocked me from my conscience mind." She found a business card from a VP with Wilshire Records. On another piece of paper, he had scratched something about Wonder Bread and motor oil, at the bottom there was a phone number with the name Darrell. Under the name and number was scratched "CD producer."

She stroked his hair as he fell back asleep. It must have been one hell of a show.

***

Waking after a solid twelve hours of sleep, not counting the six-hour car ride from the Keys, Jack still felt surprisingly rough. He crawled out of bed, pulled on a t-shirt and a pair of shorts, and saw Janie sitting out on the patio with a cup of coffee. He poured a cup for himself and joined her.

"Good morning," she said with a smile. "How are you feeling?"

"I think with a little luck, and a lot of coffee, I just might pull through."

Janie put her hand on his arm. "You must have had a good time. How was your show?"

"The show at Schooner's was over the top," he said with a big smile. "People danced, they bought us drinks, they requested an encore. It was great! I think I picked up a couple of shows around the country. I talked with people from Oklahoma, Omaha, even Montana and Washington State. The Parrothead clubs from those states seem to be thirsty for what we're serving. I think with a little planning, I could put together a pretty cool tour."

Janie frowned slightly. "You've got a pretty good thing going here. Do you really want to take it on the road to places like Missoula and Seattle? The road seems like a place that could be lonely as hell."

Jack turned to her, and she could see the excitement in his eyes. "I talked with a guy, Michael something, he said we had the right sound. He loved my lyrics. He wanted to sign me to a recording contract. Another guy offered to produce a CD for me.

I found a lady who could build a website, and got a lead on a company that does custom t-shirts and hats.

"I had a beer with a guy down there who said the formula to success is pretty simple. Write new material, release a new album every twelve months, and keep playing shows to build your fan base. He said that if a guy builds a solid base of a thousand rabid fans, that translates into an income of a hundred thousand dollars a year. I've never put a number to it. I've always figured that if I'm having fun, I got more than my money's worth."

She was thrilled that Jack was so excited. He went on about recording albums and possibly playing a festival on Chesapeake Bay. The more he talked, the more she imagined her love life taking place over late night phone calls from places she had never been. But she was in love, and she vowed to herself that morning, there on the patio, that she would support him and his career, wherever it led them.

Jack purchased the biggest whiteboard calendar he could find and nailed it to the wall in the spare bedroom, which became his office. His desk was a folding table and a kitchen chair. The calendar quickly began to fill up with shows scheduled in Tampa, Orlando, and as far away as Mobile and Tallahassee. He contacted the studio producer he had met in Key West and they discussed the logistics and cost of recording a CD. Jack was floored by the expense but knew if he was going to be a big rock star, he was going to have to somehow make it happen.

The solution to finance the CD was simple, yet painful. He walked over to the *Marauder* and crawled aboard her as she sat on the boat lift behind Richard's house. She was big and beautiful. Her twin Merc engines had been running flawlessly. He loved her, and he wasn't sure he could ever let her go. Even thinking about it made him feel like he was being unfaithful to her.

A strange sense of reality sometimes caught Jack off guard. Emotionally, he wasn't prepared to let her go, but he hadn't taken the *Marauder* out in a couple of weeks, mainly due to time and money. She drank an incredible amount of fuel and his schedule, between bartending, playing, and fishing, kept him pretty busy. He bought her to use for his own charter fishing venture, which he had never gotten off the ground. She was an expensive toy that he couldn't really afford to own.

"How's the fishing?" came a voice from behind him.

Jack spun around to see Richard, his wife Pam, and their little dog, Mango, on the walk next to the waterway. "I haven't caught a damn thing all morning."

"Well, you probably know more about fishing than I do, but it seems to me that you'd catch more if you had a line in the water," said Richard.

Jack laughed. "That's sage advice. Next time, I'll give that a try."

Richard and Pam gave a wave as they walked their dog down the waterway. Jack reminded himself that if it wasn't for their generosity, he would have another expense he couldn't afford.

CHAPTER SIXTEEN

Bar Stools and Beach Chairs

Five days later, Roger and Stephanie, a retired firefighter and his wife, were all smiles as they idled away in the *Marauder*. Jack was left holding a big cashier's check and the dream of one day owning a boat again. He called the studio and booked time and background musicians.

Three weeks later, he arrived at the studio in Cocoa Beach completely unprepared to record an album. There was no manual, no instructions, no Idiot's Guide to Recording Your First Album. When Darrell, the owner of the studio, asked him for the sheet music for the backup band, Jack gave him a blank stare. When he asked for the list of songs that Jack planned to put on the album, Jack pulled out one of his trusty yellow legal pads and started writing them down. Then he started drawing arrows to change the order of the songs. Darrell asked if the album had a name, or a cover tune, or album liners, song liners, cover art, and a number of other items. Jack admitted those were all great questions, but questions he couldn't answer.

Jack wrote background music in bed, in his car, in the night, in the morning, and in-between. He wrote a great song in the shower, but the water smeared the words. He tried to write in the studio, but the musicians kept making too much noise. Eventually he got it done, and he realized that he really liked writing songs. He told himself that he needed to do it more often.

After two weeks of messing with sonic marvelizers, loudifiers, clestorted guitars, sklarb settings, sloov buttons, gotars and compresticators, they emerged victorious from their battle with sonic debris. At the end, Chris, the lead guitarist turned to Jack, a little misty-eyed, and said, "Thanks to your vision, some nights we worked really late, and some nights we never went home."

Jack wasn't sure it was a compliment, but as he left the studio, Darrell shook his hand and said he was looking forward to producing his next album.

From Cocoa Beach, he headed northwest towards Daphne, Alabama, where he was scheduled to play a house party. The last day at the studio had run long. He would have to drive all night to make the show. He stopped in a convenience store parking lot in Perry, Florida for a couple of hours, then made it to downtown Apalachicola, where he got a little more sleep before the morning traffic woke him up. He finally found a deserted beach on Cape San Blas, where he got some meaningful rest in his beach chair. He made it to Alabama just in time to play the house party.

He was warmly greeted at the home of Ron and Loretta Raines, a couple he had met at one of his regular shows at Bert's. They spent the evening listening to him, and when he finished, he had two new fans and a request to play at an annual party they threw. Their home and backyard were fantastic, with nearly an acre of grass overlooking Mobile Bay. They treated him like a celebrity, introducing him to all of their friends, making him feel like a semi-significant star rather than the hired help. They all helped carry his gear to a gazebo that would act as his stage, then they made sure he had all the delicious food and cold Coronas he could possibly need.

When he was sufficiently full and had two beers down with another in his hand, he turned towards his host and said, "Let's get this party started!" The crowd of about a hundred and fifty people applauded as he took the stage. After his first set, they applauded and cheered louder.

During his break, somebody asked the all too familiar question, "Do you have an album we can buy?"

He could finally, proudly answer, "I just finished recording my first CD. It will be available in a couple of weeks." Before he packed up to leave for the evening, he had a list of twenty-three pre-ordered CDs and a pocket full of cash.

In negotiating the show with Ron Raines, he had tossed out a number that for the first time included a hotel room, gas money, and a few hundred bucks for the concert. Ron had readily agreed. Then his gracious host even passed around a tip jar. Jack piled the money from the CD sales and the tip jar on the bed of his hotel room and started counting. He smiled. The all-night drive, sleeping in the car, and bad food at convenience stores was suddenly all worth it. He called Janie and told her about the hundreds of dollars that now sat in neat piles on the bed. "I think I fooled them again!"

Janie was always happy to take his late-night calls, and she was even happier when he was excited. She could tell from his voice that he was tired. "You're not still planning to go to Luckenbach, are you?"

There was a pause before Jack said, "I don't know. I'm beat."

Jack had conjured up a crazy plan. After finishing up at the studio and driving to Alabama, he figured he was within striking distance of Fredericksburg, Texas, where one of his musical idols and greatest influences, Jerry Jeff Walker, was playing the following evening at the Luckenbach Dance Hall. Jack had listened to his music for years but had never had the opportunity to see him play live. Janie worried that he was pushing himself too hard. "Why don't you get a good night's sleep and come home tomorrow? We'll check his schedule and find a show near us and go see him together."

He hung up the phone after assuring her he would get some sleep and see how he felt in the morning. He set an alarm and crawled into bed. As he fell asleep, he heard Janie's concerned voice, then he heard Jerry Jeff singing his favorite songs: "L.A. Freeway," "Sangria Wine," "Contrary to Ordinary," and "Navajo Rug."

Keeping his promise to Janie that he would see how he felt in the morning, when the alarm went off at 6am, he woke, got out of bed, and stretched. He felt good, given he only had a few hours of sleep under his belt. He brushed his teeth, pulled on a ball cap, and pointed the car west towards the Luckenbach Dance Hall.

Jerry Jeff Walker had been one of Jack's favorite Texas singer/songwriters since he was a kid. Jack liked his music, but his real fascination came from his lyrics. Jerry Jeff was a storyteller who had an amazing ability to craft his lines and rhymes like no other. Jack had always wanted to see Jerry Jeff play live, but their paths had never crossed. Now he was just ten or twelve hours away from not only a chance to see one of his idols, but a chance to see him play in one of the classic Texas music venues.

To make it in time for the show, he would have to break one of his cardinal rules; he wouldn't be taking the road by the water. He hoped the gods of the sands and the seas would forgive him this one time. He chewed up the road, flying down I-10 through Baton Rouge, Lafayette, and Lake Charles. He hit Houston and luckily made it through without any significant traffic delays. Cruising up US-290, he saw lots of great country that he would have loved to explore, but he kept his nose pointing west. He skimmed south of Austin, and an hour and a half later, he pulled into the parking lot of the huge dance hall.

Jack was bone tired but running on adrenaline as he paid at the door. The hall was packed, but luckily, he found a table, not too far from the front, but far right of the stage.

Sitting at a table in front of him was a pretty brunette woman who Jack guessed was about twenty years older than himself. Just before the show started, a couple of other ladies sat with her, who appeared to be with the band. Looking again, he recognized the brunette as Susan Walker, Jerry Jeff's wife. He was too shy to introduce himself to her.

The band played all his favorite songs. He knew them all by heart and sang along with most of them. When the show ended,

Jack tried to follow the ladies backstage, acting like he was with them, but the bouncer stopped him. He wouldn't get the chance to meet Jerry Jeff, but little did he know, eventually his day would come.

He slept in his car in the parking lot of an out of business furniture store until the sun woke him, then he started east towards home. As Jack drove towards the rising sun, he thought about his life and contrasted the reality with his dreams. He was tired, he was really tired.

The greasy truck-stop pizza he had eaten for breakfast had been a big mistake. It made him feel twice his age. He was a little one-man circus, living like a gypsy. He wondered how long he could live like this, sleeping in the back seat of his car, eating bad food, enduring late-night concerts and early morning drives from place to place.

After a quick four-hour stop in the French Quarter, he felt good enough to keep moving east for a few hours. Taking the road by the water, he chose US-90, crossing Bay St. Louis to Pass Christian where he decided he was hungry and his butt hurt. On the gulf side of the road, he found Shaggy's, a cool-looking beach joint.

The sign on the door said, "Entertainment Tonight," but when he asked, the waitress said she didn't think they had anybody scheduled to play. Jack ordered a beer and asked to speak to the manager. When Candice, the manager, arrived at his table, he did his best to convince her he was a talented musician and offered to play for two hours in exchange for dinner and a couple of beers.

"How do I know you're any good?" she asked.

Jack smiled at her. "Let me play one song. If you don't like it, give me a thumbs-down and I'll pack up and leave."

"That sounds fair," she said. "How about an appetizer to get you started?"

After a couple of fish tacos to hold him over, he retrieved his guitar from the car and hooked into their amps. He stepped up to the microphone, and without an introduction, started singing "Southward." Two couples sitting at a table just off the stage stopped talking and turned to listen.

Suddenly, it was all worth it. The long hours of hamburger-butt driving, the late nights and early mornings, being stuck in rush hour traffic, breakfasts at the Waffle House and dinners at the Circle K, and the days and days away from Janie. Everything was forgotten when he stepped up to that microphone on the stage. Despite it all, Jack was having the time of his life.

As he finished "Southward," a tall man and his wife approached the stage with big smiles. "Hey, Jack," said the man. "Remember us?" he said as he pushed out his hand. "Jens and Shelly from Biloxi. We met you down at The Ice House in Florida!"

Jack didn't really remember them but told them how good it was to see them again. They said they were surprised and excited to see him playing at Shaggy's and then they requested that one song, the one with that one line, "if it doesn't work out, that's the way it goes."

Jack looked towards the bar and caught Candice smiling at him with two thumbs-up. He turned back to the microphone. "Okay, by request from Jens and Shelly, 'Laid Back and Key Wasted.'"

"Several years ago, the company I worked for asked me to move to North Dakota. They offered me lots of money, a promotion, even a possible partnership in the firm. It was an amazing opportunity, but I decided instead of going north to design and engineer oil fracking sites in the wind and snow, that I'd quit and move south so I could write and play songs for you guys. I wrote this song about that decision."

He finished the evening with seven pre-order requests for his new CD, a number of people who promised to watch for its release on his website, and a return date on his calendar to play

Shaggy's for money. Jens and Shelly wanted him to play in Biloxi, and Candice bought his dinner. He loaded up, excited to get home, and he drove as far east as he could.

After crossing Mobile Bay, he got off the freeway and started looking for a place to pull over and sleep. Nothing looked as pretty as that Florida welcome sign, he thought as he drove into Paradise Beach. He followed a road south to the Blue Angel Recreation Area and slept in the parking lot next to a "No Camping or Overnight Parking" sign. The sun rose, making it too hot to sleep in the car any longer, so he took his old green beach chair out of the back and walked down to the water. He dozed in his chair for another hour with his feet stuck in Perdido Bay.

With the sun shining hot on his face, he forced himself to wake up. Sitting there, he smiled as he remembered the roar of the small but enthusiastic crowd from Shaggy's. He played for beer and food, and slept in parking lots and rest areas while driving the backroads. He was paying all the dues, but despite it all, playing in salty old bars and sleeping in cars, it was a pretty good job.

Jack moved his chair to the shade of a tree and got a yellow pad out of his car. He jotted down a few notes about his so-called job, and a half hour later, he was looking at the start of a pretty good song. He was hundreds of miles from home, but he had a beautiful view of the bay. He would drive all day along the water to get back to Janie, but tomorrow, he knew he would find a place to fish and drink cold beer with his friends. Then he would be back on a barstool, playing his songs to a small but growing fan base around Charlotte Harbor. Today was just another day at the office for him, and he felt damn lucky to live his life that way.

After returning home, and while waiting for his CD to arrive, Jack spent two weeks engaged in intense research, looking for song ideas for his second CD. At least that was how he explained his bawdy and outrageous behavior to Janie. His research included lots of fishing, hours lying on the beach, some late nights with friends, and drinking enough to forget the words to his own songs while playing a show at Bert's. Janie was a good sport, and she knew he had worked hard to record the album and that in his own way, he was simply recharging his batteries.

Sunday finally rolled around and with it came an invite from Dennis and Nancy for a trip out to Pelican Pass for a beach party on Cayo Costa. Jack asked who was going to be there and what they should bring. Dennis answered with a wave of his hand, "Don't worry who's invited, don't worry what to bring. It's a Sunday party island soiree wing ding sort of thing."

Dennis and Nancy picked them up at the dock and they motored out to the island. There were already at least ten boats at the beach when they arrived, a civilized invasion of the unnamed sandbar. As they eased towards the beach, Dennis warned, "This party's not for sissies. There's gonna be some drinking and there just might be no clothes." Nancy rolled her eyes while asking her husband to keep his shorts on.

Frank was at the barbecue grilling chicken wings. Mark was using his new gas-powered blender to make rum drinks. Between the noisy batches of blended drinks, Jack played his guitar. Shannon estimated they had enough food for a week, but Gil was worried that they might run out of alcohol before sunset. Dale volunteered to lead a mission to get more beer before tripping over a beach chair and landing on a blanket in the arms of LeAnn. The mission was scrubbed.

As the day warmed, most of them ended up waist-deep in the water with a cooler of beer floating between them, telling jokes and sharing stories. Jack tossed an empty can up on the beach near a growing pile of dead soldiers and yelled to his buddy standing closest to the cooler, "Hey, Randy, my koozie's empty." A beer was quickly delivered via airmail. Jack tried to soak it all in. He wanted to remember every moment; every bit of it was a future song.

Dennis yelled out that it was time to do community drinks. Everybody participated in the local ritual. After a number of drinks, Dennis yelled again that it was time for everybody to try the naked watermelon dance. Janie looked frightened, but Nancy just laughed.

As Jack and Janie retreated to a pair of beach chairs to watch the shenanigans from a safer spot, Carla handed them a couple of fresh rum drinks. Jack felt an overwhelming sense of calm come over him as he sat there, so far from roads and traffic, so far from corporate America, world news, and war and violence.

Looking around, he realized how lucky he was. He had sunny skies, salty air, miles and miles of beach with clear water everywhere. He had a girl who said she loved him and a cold drink made with some fine Jamaican rum. He swore he would be happy until the end of time. He just hoped that it would never come.

He turned to Janie and "clinked" his red Solo cup against hers, saying, "I think I want to die from relaxation with a rum drink in my hand."

She smiled at him. "I'll remember that line for you."

Jack looked at the beautiful woman sitting next to him. She was everything to him. He loved to watch her from a distance. She moved so free and easy, it took his breath away. They had experienced their ups and downs, and he almost lost her when he left the Keys. Now he couldn't imagine his life without her. She had become his rock, his foundation. She was the solid Yin to his crazy and fluid Yang lifestyle. When the world got too crazy, she was always there to pick him up.

"You know the whole world is crazy, except me and you," he said while watching Dennis and some others doing a crazy butt dance down by the water. "But every day or two, I'm not so sure about you."

She gave him a sassy smile. "You're such a funny man."

"You know, I really am," replied Jack with a big smile. "If I asked you someday," he said after a few moments, "do you think you'd marry me?"

Janie laughed and snorted and gave him a familiar punch on the shoulder. "Well, yeah! I made up my mind months ago."

Smiling back at her, he said, "That's good to know. I'll have to remember to ask you some day."

She gave him a big smile. Her smile was always like that time on a cloudy day when the sun finally came shining through.

***

The doorbell rang a little after two the next afternoon. Jack opened the door to find a UPS driver standing next to three medium-sized boxes. He excitedly scratched his name on line 42 of the man's clipboard, resisted his urge to hug the driver, and then moved the boxes inside. He tore open one of the boxes and held a copy of his first shrink-wrapped CD in his hands.

It was an indescribable feeling, holding his first album. The thousands of hours he had put into practicing, playing, and writing, the endless driving, playing to tiny audiences, bad food, sleeping in cars, and hauling heavy equipment, all seemed worthwhile. He didn't feel like a bartender with a guitar anymore; he felt like a musician.

He wrestled the cellophane wrapping off the CD he held, found a sharpie, wrote an inscription, and headed for his Jeep. Janie was surprised to see him walk into her office. He was smiling out loud.

"Jack! What are you doing here?"

He handed her the CD. She held it as if she was holding a rare book. "Oh my god, Jack, it turned out amazing." She opened the case and read the inscription. She smiled, wiped a tear from her eye, and said, "Of course I'll marry you."

***

The initial order of one thousand CDs sold quickly. Jack sent out the forty-three pre-ordered CDs, the Nav-A-Gator asked for twenty to sell, then another twenty after a week. Bert's, the Ice House, two local book stores, and a coffee shop all started selling his album. He sold ten to twenty each time he played and with his website up, he found that he was spending much more time than he had anticipated answering emails and fulfilling online orders. He placed a second order for a thousand CDs just a month after receiving his first order.

Songs for the second album were nearly complete and he had booked time at the studio a few months out. He felt like he could easily make his goal of releasing his second album within a year of the first.

Something had changed since the release of the CD and the website. Across Southern Florida, there were hundreds of people who played their guitars in the funky little beach bars that dotted the area, he was just another. But once he recorded an album and had it available at his shows and on his website, he felt a higher level of respect from those who didn't know him or didn't know him well. He felt like a more substantial artist. Maybe it was the way people perceived him, but maybe it was the way he projected himself.

His bookings for shows increased, and he started to feel more like a travel agent than a performer. The requests to play started coming from further away, and he soon had shows booked up and down the Eastern Seaboard and around the Gulf Coast. He also noticed a growing popularity in the Pacific Northwest, an area he referred to as "The Land of Long Pants." Jack had requests coming from Seattle and Boise, even Montana.

Jack's life was quickly becoming something he hadn't anticipated. His world had become driving to the airport at 4:30 AM, checking gear, paying baggage fees, waiting in security lines, dealing with TSA, delayed flights, crowded planes, surly flight attendants, sitting next to a huge guy with a hacking cough who spilled into his seat, waiting for baggage, missing baggage, rental cars, bad hotel rooms, and 6:00 AM return flights.

But in the middle of all his pain and suffering, Jack would get to step out on a stage and kick off his shoes where it was all forgotten. He would be singing his songs, the crowd would sing along, that was the life that he loved. He was getting paid to hang out in bars, singing his songs and carrying on like a semi-significant star. Everybody showed up happy and nobody ever wanted to leave. Jack joked from behind the microphone that he had bar front property wherever he went. It was a pretty cool job.

***

Jack dreaded the bachelor party that seemed so important to Dennis and Randy. He imagined the backroom at Bert's full of hookers, his friends force feeding him shot after shot until he puked or did something stupid, probably both. Janie and her friends were going to Tampa to take in a play and spend some time being pampered in a spa. Jack thought that sounded much nicer than strippers and tequila.

When the evening arrived, Dennis picked Jack up and drove him down to Fisherman's Wharf. Randy, Bernard, Jimi, John, and a couple of other friends were waiting on Ed's boat. They handed him a cold beer as they left the dock.

"So what kind of drunken debauchery have you cooked up?" Jack asked with a roll of his eyes.

"You said you didn't want the typical bachelor party, so you're not getting one," said Dennis as they idled through the marina. "We thought you'd enjoy an evening of drinking beer with your friends around a campfire out on Cabbage Key."

Jack smiled and let out a big sigh. "That sounds perfect!"

Their wedding was a party and Jack didn't have to perform. He wasn't exactly sure how to behave. It had been a long time since he had been to a party where he didn't have a guitar hanging from his shoulder. It seemed that everybody they had met in the area was there, including Pearl and Eddy, who showed up with their new baby. Bill and Jenny came from St. Louis, Vido and Jodi blew in, John and Kathy from the bed and breakfast in Key West brought a carload of friends up for the fun.

Taking a page from Eddie and Pearl's beach wedding, they threw a big party. Sunny Jim played along with Jack's Fish Head band, Amy passed around Jell-O shots, Dennis made multiple toasts to the happy couple. When everybody was fed and happy, Sunny Jim asked everybody to fill their drinks, announcing that Janie and Jack were ready to exchange their vows.

The ceremony, led by Reverend Misty, would have lasted about fifteen minutes, but with a gleam in her eye, she said, "If anybody knows of any reason these two should not be wed, speak now or forever hold your peace." A line formed and the wedding turned into a hilarious Jack and Janie roast. For the next thirty minutes, friend after friend shared sidesplitting reasons why the happy couple shouldn't marry. The two laughed at the comedic speeches until they cried. They partied late into the night, and Jack and Janie were amongst the last to leave.

Janie surprised Jack with a honeymoon on Isla Mujeres, a little island off Mexico's Yucatan Peninsula. She found a bargain at a little resort called Villa Rolandi, one of the top ten small resorts in the world, where normally the rooms were eight hundred dollars a night. In the off-season, they were incredibly inexpensive.

On their first day at the resort, they decided to spend some time at the beach. They put on their swimsuits and loaded a bag with sunscreen, bug spray, towels, and cameras, then headed down towards the water. A staff member stopped them along the path, telling them that the beach was closed for the day. Playboy magazine was doing a photo shoot. But since they were inconvenienced, they would be welcome to watch if they liked. Jack readily agreed. Janie shrugged her shoulders and followed along.

After spending an hour watching the photographer trying to get the perfect shot of a beautiful, naked woman in a waterfall with a conch shell between her legs, Janie said she was going to walk into the village to do some shopping. She asked if Jack was interested in going with her. Jack looked at her and said, "No, I think I'll just sit here and guard the Yucatan." She laughed as she walked away. He had that look in his eye; he found a piece of paper and a pen in their beach bag and was voraciously making notes. She smelled a new song coming.

They enjoyed a very relaxing week on Isla Mujeres and agreed they would have to come back. A week was simply too short of a time at such an amazing place. Returning to Punta Gorda, Janie fell back into her routine and Jack fell back into what was becoming routine to him. His travel continued to increase, more shows and more time away from home. Recording his second album went much smoother than the first. He arrived at the studio better prepared and they religiously followed the three C's of recording: coffee, cookies, and Coronas.

CHAPTER SEVENTEEN

The Road

Everybody rushed the last day of recording so Jack could get home in time to unload his suitcase, reload his suitcase, and get four hours of sleep before driving to the airport for a flight to Seattle. He arrived in Seattle just in time to have a bite to eat before playing at the local Parrothead Club's annual golf tournament, the Tin Cup Chalice.

The following day, Ron and Cindy gave him a tour of the cool non-touristy areas of the greater Seattle area before he played a house concert at Karen and Gordy's home. The party was called "The Church of Good Tequila" after one of Jack's songs.

Karen talked Jack into donning a Pope's costume and asked him to give a "blessing" to start the party. "Just make something up," she told him.

Standing in front of the crowd, he put up his hands in a very divine manner and prayed as reverently as he could. "When God made man, he made him out of string. He had a little left over, so he left a little thing. When God made woman, he made her out of lace. He didn't have enough, so he left a little place."

The audience howled at his antics. He baptized his congregation with beer and yelled, "Let the festivities began!" Jack had a great time playing his first ever "church" party. He stayed up too late and drank too much.

The next day, he nursed his hangover at a brunch with Bloody Marys before it was time to get to the airport. That evening, he played in Boise to a small but very enthusiastic group of fans who surprised him by singing along with most of his songs. He readily accepted an offer to spend the next day fly fishing on the Owyhee River.

His gracious hosts dropped him at the airport the following morning, where he rented a car and started the long drive to Bozeman, Montana. He had all day, so he explored, stopping here and there and enjoying the scenery. By evening, it was clear he wasn't going to make it to Bozeman before dark, which was fine with him.

After driving along the Madison River for several miles, he came into the little town of Cameron and parked in front of the Blue Moon Saloon. On a whim, and always looking to save a buck or two while also building his fan base, he grabbed a CD from the box in the backseat before going in where he found a barstool and a cold beer.

The manager, on seeing that he had recorded a CD, quickly agreed to Jack's proposal, a steak and some beer in return for two hours of live music. After a delicious T-bone, Jack played his guitar to six tired cowboys, a girl named Cheyenne, two dogs, and a skunk drunk old man. He sold a CD to Cheyenne and traded another to the manager in exchange for a Blue Moon Saloon hat.

As he packed up to leave, he found a picture that Janie had given him. It was of the two of them sitting on Randy's sailboat. He missed her. The winds whipped around him as he wrestled his suitcase and guitar towards a small and rustic cabin he had rented for the night. He pulled the collar of his light jacket around his neck trying to fend off the wind, while thinking to himself, how could anybody live in a place like this?

When they spoke the previous night, Janie told him she was going out for a Friday night sail with some of her friends. As he battled to get the electric heater in the cabin to work, he could picture her sailing on a warm ocean breeze. In his cabin, it felt like it was sixteen degrees.

He missed being where the air was thick and the palm trees grew. Janie had warned him that the road would be lonely as hell. Looking at the picture of his new bride drove him wild. He missed her, he missed home. He was learning the lesson of the road so well.

By morning, the winds had died and the sky was absolutely cloudless. It was still far too cold for his liking, but he couldn't deny the amazing beauty of the area. After breakfast, he scraped the windows of his little rental car and started the relatively short drive to Bozeman, enjoying both the snowcapped mountains and the heat blowing from the vents of his car.

He played that night for the Bozeman Parrothead club at the Eagles Lodge. They purchased every CD he had remaining in the cardboard box he had been carrying around with him. They bought him drinks, requested his songs, sang along with a few of them, and asked how soon he was coming back. He had to admit, he was developing a love/hate relationship with the road, but he promised them he would be back, especially if his return trip included some fly fishing. Rick Clemons stepped up, saying, "That's a deal!"

***

Two days later, tired and ready for some down time, Jack made the forty-minute drive from the Fort Meyers airport, arriving home just before dark. Parked in the driveway of their little house was an older, yellow, 16-foot Hewes Bonefisher flats boat with a 90-horse Yamaha outboard. From the street, he could see a red bow taped to the console. An envelope with his name on it was taped next to the bow. He set down his suitcase and guitar and curiously opened the envelope.

The card read: "Congratulations on your wedding, Happy Birthday and Merry Christmas for the next twenty years. Love Janie, Dennis and Nancy, Ed, Randy, Bernard, Eddie and Pearl, the bar flies at the Ice House, the tip jar from the Nav-A-Gator, and several adoring fans. Now go write us all some new songs on your boat!"

Jack looked at the boat, read the card again, then hearing a sound behind him, turned to find Janie leading about twenty of his closest friends out on to the front lawn. They let up a big cheer.

Janie rushed to him and hugged him, saying, "It was Dennis and Nancy's idea."

Dennis stepped forward. "How could a guy that sings about and fishing and boats not own one of his own? So we all went in and bought you one. It's not much, but it will get you out on the water where you can fish and spend time doing what you do best, making shit up."

"Eddie went over her from top to bottom," said Janie. "He said she's as good a new...until something breaks."

Eddie gave a shy smile, and he kicked the ground, saying, "She's solid."

For the first time in his life, Jack was speechless.

***

Jack couldn't talk Janie into taking the day off to try out his new boat. Everybody he knew was busy, but that was okay, there was nothing better than a day out on the water alone.

It was hard to beat the quiet stillness of the morning. Jack stretched out on his boat drifting just off Useppa, heading wherever the breeze wanted him to go.

It was one of those special days, a day when he had no place to be and no one to count on him. It was the type of day that had become rare but a day that he learned to appreciate more and more as his career grew, a day when the world seemed to turn very slow. He didn't fish, he just lay on the deck and thought about life for a while.

It had taken him a while and he wondered how he had ever come this far. He had worked pretty damn hard but reminded himself that his "play job" was incredibly cool. He got paid to hang out in bars, to play his guitar at fun parties, and to sing to lots of really cool people. He made a living by staying up late, carousing with his friends and fans, and turning those nights into stories.

He never would regret all the time he spent hanging out in a bar. His music and his career was based on all the stuff he had seen, and it had taken him pretty damn far. Those funky old joints sure had had treated him well. When he showed up to play, the drinks were all free and the owners knew him by name.

He was just a writer guy who played the guitar, always looking for something to say. A day on his boat was a pretty good day at work, and he knew he was lucky to live life this way.

CHAPTER EIGHTEEN

Eye of the Storm

Janie didn't expect Jack to be home when she got off work. She knew he would be on the water until dark and maybe even after. He had a new toy and he had been absolutely giddy with excitement to take his new boat out. He had gotten out of bed before her to get it ready for a day on the water.

The phone call wasn't from Jack; it was from Deputy Somebody at the Charlotte County Sheriff's Department. They had found an empty boat registered to her, drifting off the Cape Haze Preserve. A preliminary search of the area had come up empty.

She laughed nervously while biting her lower lip. She told the deputy that her guess was he was wading the flats, fishing somewhere nearby, and his boat got loose. With an hour of daylight left, the sheriff's department decided to launch a helicopter search. They would call her back shortly.

Janie called Dennis, Mark, and Randy, asking them to get on the water and head for Cape Haze to help find Jack. They all dropped what they were doing and headed for their boats. "It's what Jack would do for any of us," said Randy.

Dennis laughed, telling her he would call her as soon as he found him, sitting on some sandbar with a stupid look on his face. "He'll never live this one down," chuckled Dennis.

Nancy came over to the house to sit with her, waiting for the call saying that they had found him. Janie raced to the window every time a car came down their street.

At midnight, Nancy put on a pot of coffee. She tried to convince Janie that if they hadn't found him by now, they probably wouldn't until daylight. "You know he's just sitting on some tiny spit of land up some little channel that they can't see in the dark. And Jack's smart enough to not try to walk out at night."

Janie put on a third pot of coffee as the sun started to rise. By 7am, word was spreading, and concerned friends started arriving at the house. News came that the Coast Guard was joining the search. More boats, more friends hit the water, and somebody said it looked like a fiberglass armada was invading the Cape Haze Preserve. The search started expanding, and soon they were looking from El Jobean to Bokeelia.

Dennis arrived at the house just before noon. He was exhausted from a long, sleepless, and frustrating night of searching. "He's got to be there, we've got to be close to him," he said with shake of his head. "We've looked up every creek, searched every mangrove, and checked every sandbar, except for the one that he's actually on."

He looked at Janie and could see the fear and doubt in her eyes. "We'll find him, Janie. I know we'll find him soon."

Janie walked out in the backyard for a few minutes of solitude away from all the noise and people. It was a sunny morning; the weather was perfect. She looked up at the blue sky. It was amazing how quickly life could change. One minute life had been easy, and the world had looked good, and the morning sun had been shining down on them. Then the colors of the day, turn from blue to gray, and in a flash, all her fears were coming true.

What would she do if they didn't find him, or if they found him and the outcome wasn't good? She pressed those thoughts back into the deep recesses of her mind. She wiped the tears from her face, stood up straight, and walked confidently back into the house.

Another long night came and went, followed by another long and painfully slow day. Janie had to do something. She had to get out of the house. She joined Randy on his boat out on the western edge of an ever-expanding search area. Storm clouds gathered on the horizon and started pushing towards them. As the winds began to swirl, it was starting to become clear to Janie that once again something mighty had made a right-hand turn into her world.

***

The official search ended after a week. They hadn't turned up anything, not even a piece of clothing. Jack's group of friends kept searching for weeks, but the results were the same.

Janie found herself standing in the wreckage of their hopes and dreams, finding it hard to see a better day. In a flash, all the things she had taken for granted seemed so far away, and all her other worries seemed so small.

Her life became a blur of search logistics, charts, and maps. She canceled bookings, canceled airline tickets and hotel rooms. She had to quickly learn the accounting of his small business, paying bills, and answering calls and emails from concerned friends and fans.

Searching his computer for a billing invoice one morning, she found a file called "Stories yet to be told." She opened it and found a long list of files that seemed to be an electronic version of the pieces of paper that he had collected with song ideas written on them. She opened a file named "Janie."

"If you're reading this, you're either snooping around in my computer (shame on you), or something bad has happened to me. I'll assume that I died of clogged arteries from too many late nights and an unending diet of beer and donuts, ice cream, and pumpkin pie (shame on me).

If I'm truly gone, and you're staring at the eye of the storm, I know you can carry on, I know your spirit will keep you strong. I love you, Janie, and I hope you've never doubted that. I want you to know my love is real.

Wherever I've gone, I'll wait for you to join me. When you get here, I'll be saving you a beach chair with an incredible view of the ocean. I'll sing you some new songs I wrote about you while you enjoy a cool margarita. I'll be excited to tell you about my days, out on the Gulf Stream, trolling for mermaids while singing my songs to the sea. I'll introduce you to the Cosmic Magician, the guy I like to think drives this rock, the guy who can finally explain to me why we we're here to begin with.

It going to be an amazing day, and an amazing reunion when you join me on the other side. I'll hold you tight, and I'll promise you, for the last time, that I will never leave you again."

ABOUT THE AUTHOR

Jim Morris was an articulate singer/songwriter with a devotion to storytelling. Whether a thoughtful ballad about doomed love or an anthem to a night of drunken revelry, the listener can always count on well-crafted songs with carefully drawn characters, clever lyrics, and satirical charm.

In the early '90's, Jim quit his corporate career to pursue his music. His fans, once stretching across all of Florida, soon followed him from around the world. As his fan base grew, he spread his wings, playing shows from Belize to Tahiti, around the U.S., Canada, and the Caribbean.

Unfortunately, in July of 2016, while touring with his band in Seattle, Jim died suddenly. His music and his legacy, however, refuse to die, carried on by his band and thousands of rabid fans.

Jim's twenty-seven albums, filled mostly with original music he wrote while staked out on a beach or floating on his boat, continue to thrill his fans and inspire the hundreds of musicians who follow in his now well established path.

Sail on, Jim!